CHOSEN BY THE FAE

WICKED FAE BOOK 3

AMELIA SHAW

AUTHOR NOTE

There are some dark scenes in this book that include torture (Chapter 4) and may trigger some readers. Please read at your own discretion.

CHAPTER 1

AURELIA

I ran through the tunnels with the help of the trees that were giving me the correct directions.

"Shit."

What the hell just happened? Everyone that I care about was just captured by the Council. What's going to happen to them? Will they be tortured the way Ronaldo tortured me?

I shook my head to clear the doom and gloom and followed the tree roots through the tunnels that appeared in front of me like magic.

If I didn't already trust the trees, I would have been frightened of where they were taking me, but they'd saved me time and again.

A root brushed my arm, urging me on. They wanted me to get away from the hollow, but I had a feeling they wouldn't like the place I was heading.

I clutched the gold book to my chest, not wanting it out of my sight. All of this would be for nothing if I lost the book.

Could it help me rescue my friends? Probably, but not without an army at my back. All my hopes hinged on this plan. There was no plan B. If I couldn't pull this off, both realms would be doomed.

No pressure.

I needed to find my army. I couldn't rescue Grey and my father without one. Every hope I had was pinned on the dungeon having loyal soldiers ready to battle the Council for my parents and the good of Faery.

I placed a hand on the root in front of me. "Please, I need a way to the castle dungeons."

The root recoiled at my request, shaking back and forth before surging forward and pushing me back a step. It obviously didn't want me to walk into danger, but I had no choice in the matter.

"I have to. I need an army to fight the Council. Please?" I stroked the root with my fingertips.

The root nodded, like actually nodded, then a tunnel opened in front of me, and I followed quickly through the packed, damp earth.

Worry clawed at my gut for Grey and the others.

What will the council do to them? How can I save them?

I needed to stop doubting myself and become the princess they all deserved. I would rescue my father's guards and then wage war against the Council.

My dirt tunnels mixed with stones the closer I got to the castle. Still, the root waved me forward. Nervousness for me bled through the connection I had to the tree, but I couldn't let it stop me from going to the castle dungeons.

The ground sloped down the farther I went. The dirt walls

of the tunnel shifted to cracked stone, and a chill swept down my spine.

I picked my way through the dark tunnel until it came to an abrupt dead end. I spun in a circle, searching the walls for any hint of a secret door but there was nothing.

"We're deep underground but where is the way inside?" I asked the root.

It pointed up and my eyes widened at the sight of the wooden hatch above me. "That just seems like bad planning."

I jumped up, grasping the handle and a loud creak filled the quiet. I flinched at the horrible sound, praying to whatever gods were listening that no one heard it.

I'd be completely screwed if there was anyone from the Council in the dungeon.

The hatch swung down, and the root tentatively wrapped around my body. It pulsed with fear for me but lifted me into hatch anyway. Crates were stacked in front of me as I pulled myself the rest of the way out and stroked the root, giving it a trickle of power in thanks for saving me.

Reaching into the darkness once more, I pulled the hatch closed. The ghastly creaking didn't sound this time, and I thanked the fates for small mercies.

The silence in the dungeon was eerie. Not even the sound of shuffling rodents' feet scratching through the walls could be heard.

Where is everyone? Surely, there can't be prisoners here?

It was just way too quiet. I crept through the crates stacked high hiding my presence and searched the cells anyway. The stench of rotting food hit me like a ton of bricks, and I nearly gagged.

There had been prisoners here, but they were gone. Where did they take them? Had my father's enemies been released?

The torches on the walls emitted an eerie glow in the darkened dungeon, throwing shadows along the walls and floor.

One cell sat open like the occupant had left in a hurry, not even bothering to close it as they ran for freedom.

Is that what happened here? Did the Council free them all to wreak havoc on the realm, or was it something worse?

I jumped when a thump sounded somewhere above me. My heart raced and panic clawed at me as stomping footsteps raced down the stairs.

Who is in my father's castle, and why would they come down here?

I hurried back to the hatch and hid behind the stacked crates, holding my breath so that I didn't make the slightest sound.

The metal door to the dungeon squeaked open, and angry voices filled the space.

"Where is she?" Ronaldo's voice boomed around me, and I flinched back against the wall.

"We've searched everywhere for the princess," a male voice replied.

A crack filled the air and a man groaned.

"The princess is in the realm. She's the only person who could have brought the mongrel through. I want her found. Now!" Ronaldo roared, and another slap rang out.

What are they doing here? Are they just looking for me? Or is it something else?

"My lord," Malcolm whispered, and I flinched.

What the hell is he doing here? He was banished just like the others.

"What is it?" Ronaldo barked.

"The princess grew up here. She was always adept at slipping away from her guards. Finding her here will be next to impossible."

"The princess lost her memories. She can't be that difficult to find," Ronaldo growled.

"Do we know for sure that she hasn't regained them somehow? We don't know how she lost her memories in the first place." Malcolm's voice softened at the end of that sentence.

"Why are you even here? You're supposed to be in the human realm enacting our plan."

"I needed to see for myself that the shifter king was captured. It's a pain in the ass that he thinks my betrothed is his mate," Malcolm said, and something hit the wall.

"You could destroy the entire plan, idiot."

"I'm the person who knew her best as a child. I know of many of her hiding places. I'll find the princess," Malcolm said.

"Did I stutter when I ordered you back to the human realm? Your role there is the most important right now. I will destroy you if you mess this up. Go. Now!" Ronaldo's voice rang out with all the authority of the pompous bastard he was.

What are they planning with the humans? Are they really working together with the human government to enslave us?

The words of the shifter that was rescued from the seemingly human jail came back to me. He didn't even know how they made him shift. There was something chemical used. Humans used chemicals, not Fae.

But why were the humans doing this to us?

The metal door to the dungeon crashed closed before two pairs of feet stormed back up to the main castle.

Ronaldo's ego knew no bounds. He didn't even bother to search the dungeon for me.

He really thought his lackeys would find me, and he didn't need to lift a finger.

Malcolm was correct that he would have been able to find me. He knew about many of the secret passages, just as I did. If Ronaldo had allowed him to search, hiding from them would have been much harder.

Silence once again rang through the stinking space. I slumped against the wall. They didn't give me anything new, just that Malcolm had an important role working with the human government on something.

That didn't sound good for us at all.

I crept out between the crates and went back to searching the cells.

I placed the book in the waistband of my jeans and opened the first cell. None of them were even locked it seemed. Father would lose his mind if he found his prisoners all gone.

There was a metal tin on the stone floor that held some sort of gruel or something that was well past its expiration date.

I plugged my nose against the stench and searched the ten-by-ten cell but found nothing that led me to who had been there.

I moved to the next cell, but there was nothing. There was no tin there with food to suggest that someone had been there.

On swift feet, I searched each individual cell, but only three had any signs that someone had occupied them. What had the Council done with the soldiers who refused to bow to them?

Had they all defected to serve the Council? Why would they? Nothing made any sense.

Had my father's army ever even been there or had this been a fool's mission from the start?

At the opposite end of the dungeon, on the wall sat a torch. It looked exactly like the others but was special as well.

The gold sconce was unassuming. The flames flickered and danced, casting light on the wall.

I pulled down on the torch and stone ground against stone as the wall opened in front of me.

Dust swirled in the air in front of me as the gears ground and opened the door wider. The musty smell in the passage tickled my nose and I held back a sneeze.

With a flick of my fingers, a cool breeze blew the dust out of the passage and away from me.

Very few knew the locations of the hidden passages in the castle, but I had found them all as a child, much to Fenrick's displeasure.

A pang of guilt prickled in my chest. Fenrick and the others were in danger, and now I was stuck in Faery with no way out and the army I had expected to be on my side was nowhere in sight.

The only thing I could do was hide and hope for a miracle.

I slipped inside the secret passage and blew out a relieved breath when the door swung shut behind me without anyone hearing me.

My eyes adjusted to the darkness in the passage as I crept down the small hall. I remembered them being so much bigger when I was a child. The walls were too close, and I panted as fear ate its way through my gut.

They were closing in on me, too small now that I was an adult. I took a deep breath through my nose and blew it out several times.

It's just a small space. It can't hurt you. The tunnels beneath the trees were small too. You got this.

No, I really didn't have this. How long was I going to have to hide in the hidden passages until I could figure out a plan?

I couldn't be seen or heard inside the castle, or someone would catch on to what I was doing.

The castle was ancient, and things creaked and groaned all too often for my taste. Especially when I played with Fenrick as a child.

Things were far more dire for me in my current situation, though. Fenrick wouldn't be the one to find me, and the punishment would be far more severe.

The Council has called for my head on multiple occasions. If they got their hands on me, it would mean my death.

CHAPTER 2

GREY

"The new realm order has already begun," Ronaldo said smugly. "And you four will be the first of the slaves."

This idiot had absolutely lost his mind. I was on my knees in front of the sadistic fuck with my hands held behind my back.

"You realize you're going to doom us all," I said.

I struggled against the guard that was holding me until the kiss of cold metal met my throat.

"Stop fighting, or you won't live long enough to be a slave. With the High Councilor's permission, I'll slit your throat," the guard at my back whispered.

"I'm not dooming us all. I'm saving us from the destruction that humanity and the unclean bring to the Fae." Ronaldo's voice was high-pitched, and his face turned red from anger.

"You doom the Fae. Humans outnumber us ten to one. You wish to go to war with them? Then you're dumber than I thought." I spat on the ground at his feet.

Just because he forced me to my knees didn't mean I had any respect for him. He never earned that. He was the reason we were dumped in the mortal world. He was the one who pretended to execute my father and kept him prisoner for centuries.

Eventually, I would watch him die.

"You wish to die, Shifter King?" Ronaldo chuckled.

The blade at my throat dug in a little but I didn't flinch at the small bite of pain. I reveled in it. I would get my revenge.

I would get revenge for whatever Aurelia suffered too.

My beautiful mate. Where was she? Did she survive the fall? I sent up a silent prayer to the gods as I stared into the eyes of evil and vowed to take him down.

"I'll tell you what," Ronaldo said, tapping his lips. "Tell me where the princess is, and I won't torture you until you can't stand."

Aurelia's father, the Shadow Fae king spoke from beside me. "You know he's a liar, Grey."

"I know. It doesn't matter though, because I don't know where she is," I said before glaring at Ronaldo.

"Last chance before you're sent back to your cesspool." Ronaldo glanced down at his fingernails as if he was bored, but I knew better.

He was very interested in where Aurelia was.

"I told you I don't know," I growled, my wolf rising to the surface with the need to kill the bastard.

"Take them through the portal. They will change their tune when I'm done with them." Ronaldo waved a hand and walked away.

Cuffs were snapped on my wrists behind my back, and I groaned as my magic was zapped out of me. "What the fuck?"

The Shadow King glanced at me, but the hilt of a sword smacked him in the back of his head.

"No talking. Don't even look at each other, or you're dead," a soldier in black armor said.

He was one of the king's warriors. How could he smack his own king and threaten him that way?

"We will get out of this!" the king bellowed. "And when we do, all you traitors will feel my wrath."

"I don't think you understand, *king*." The same guard sneered. "You are in magic-blocking cuffs on your way to becoming a slave. You've lost. We will rule all."

Is he really that delusional? He won't rule anything. He's a guard. A grunt meant to be cannon fodder.

I kept my mouth shut as the guards shoved us through the portal. I slumped my shoulders as I landed in the human world again. I'd never wanted to be back here.

Glancing behind me, I saw the portal for the first time in centuries. It really had been there the whole time. So close to my building, yet I never even knew it.

I scanned the clearing, searching for the troll I'd left on guard, but there were too many Fae around even for a troll. I hoped he ran when the Council took over the portal.

We were so close to my property it pained me. Even if I had been able to escape, I wouldn't have gone to my people. I wouldn't lead the Council's goons there. Who knew what would happen to them?

"Move, Shifter King." The guard behind me shoved me in the back and I stumbled with a growl.

The Fae King glanced at me, but I shook my head. There was no way out of this. We had to do what they said and pray to the gods Aurelia was okay and able to help us out of this.

Aurelia. My wolf howled in my mind as I thought about my missing mate. Had the fall killed her? Or was she biding her time until she could get us all out of the mess we were in?

I wanted more than anything for it to be the latter.

The guard at my back shoved me again. "What's the matter, Shifter King? You don't have anything cocky to say to me now?"

"It does no good for me to make threats now." I shrugged. "You won't win this war."

The guard laughed as he pushed me again. "Look around. We already have."

"And you call me cocky?" I smirked.

I glanced at Fenrick on my other side, but quickly turned away. His eyes were haunted. He didn't think Aurelia made it. I could tell that from the look in his eyes.

I refused to believe she was gone. The trees in Faery helped her before. I had to believe they would have helped her this time too.

"She's alive," I whispered to Fenrick. "She has to be."

My wolf would have felt it if she died, even if she wasn't officially mated to me yet. She was mine and I would feel it if she was gone.

We were forced to march through the forest to the main road.

Please don't let any of my people drive past us. They will try to save us, and there are just too many Fae soldiers.

A black van with no windows sat idling on the side of the road as we broke through the tree line.

That was fucking ominous. There was no license plate on the back of the van and nothing I could see that would identify where it had come from.

One of the guards opened the back door, which revealed two rows of bench seats inside the completely gutted van. They'd obviously been planning this.

I was shoved toward the van first and sat where they told me, at the end. The asshole guard sat next to me, his sword gripped tightly in his hand.

He eyed me warily as Magna was shoved into the seat in front of me. She frowned at the man who treated her so harshly but turned quickly away.

Her eyes gleamed with something I couldn't name, and a small smile pulled at her features.

What the hell is up with her? Is she seeing something we can't? How can she without her magic?

I glanced back at Fenrick and the Shadow King being shoved into the van, and the guard brought the hilt of his sword up under my chin. My head flew back, and it rattled my jaw. Pain washed through my skull as I hit the back of my head on the metal wal of the van behind me.

"Don't talk. Don't look at each other and keep your eyes on the floor until we get there, mongrel," the guard next to me hissed in my ear.

My wolf growled in my head at the *mongrel* comment. I would show the idiot who the real mongrel was, but that would not be today.

There was nothing I could do with my power locked down. Even if I could, it would hurt the others in the crossfire.

My mate would never forgive me if something happened to

them because of me.

I made a vow to myself then and there to see all the traitors to the crown dead before the end of the war that was coming.

It would be my mission in life to watch the motherfuckers burn. They wanted to hurt my people? They would go through me.

The van made a U-turn, and I pitched to the side into the guard next to me. He shoved me off him, and I nearly toppled to the floor. I growled at the guard, my wolf riding me hard.

He couldn't come out. I couldn't shift with the cuffs on, but the guard gulped at whatever horrors he saw in my eyes.

He saw his death, and it would be mine.

"Grey, easy," Magna mumbled, and got a slap to her face.

She turned to the guard and smiled at him even as a red handprint formed on her cheek.

That guard had just earned his death as well. Magna was not someone to be trifled with, and the evil grin on her face was testament enough to her power as a seer.

What are you planning, Magna? What have you seen?

She glanced at me like she knew what I was thinking and shook her head imperceptibly. *Right. We can't tip our hand.*

The country roads were bumpy, and with our hands tied behind our backs there was no way to keep ourselves steady. Fenrick grunted as his guard punched him in the gut for daring to touch him.

It was a mess and a great excuse for the guards to punish us.

We bumped over the roads until we came to the highway. The road evened out, but I couldn't see where we were with the partition between us and the driver. They'd made sure we were completely clueless.

Where the fuck were they taking us? The van slowed to a stop, and I trained my ears on the voice in the front of the van.

"Are these the criminals we were told the councilor was bringing in?" a rough voice asked.

"It's the High Councilor, idiot. You will be punished just like the beasts if you don't show proper respect," another deep voice drawled.

Beasts. That's what we all were to the Council. Beasts that deserved nothing more than to be slaves. I would end them all if I could right now.

"Yes, sir, the High Councilor said you had prisoners coming. I'll alert the warden. You know where to go," a rough voice said.

Were we at a human prison manned by the Fae? How the hell did Ronaldo start working so closely with the humans that they were giving him use of their facilities for those who had committed no crimes?

The van started moving again on another bumpy gravel road and I groaned as a buzzer sounded too loudly in my ears. I was startled when the clang of metal hitting metal sounded. That had to have been the gate. We were locked in, and if Ronaldo had anything to say about it, we were never getting out.

The van stopped and the doors opened, letting the too-bright sun filter into the cramped space. I was yanked by my arm out of the van and stared up at the intimidating building before me with bars on the windows.

It was exactly as I feared. They'd brought us to a maximum-security human prison. Was there even any way to get us out?

Where are you, Aurelia? I hope you have a plan to get us out of here.

CHAPTER 3

AURELIA

Memories hit me like a sledgehammer to my chest as I picked through the secret passageways in the main castle.

I had such a happy childhood until it all went wrong. Until Malcolm abducted me and set me on this path. One day he would die for those crimes against me, but for now I needed to find someone—anyone—still loyal to my father.

The passage curved up and I followed it to a small door. I needed to get into the actual castle if I was to find anyone. I pressed my hand against the wall and pushed. Metal scraped against stone as the door opened into a child's bedroom.

"Well, shit," I whispered.

They'd kept it exactly the way I left it. Why?

I crept to the four-poster bed with the bright pink comforter and ran my hand across the silk. I'd always hated the color pink, but never had the nerve to tell my mom.

She would have been so disappointed, and I didn't want her

to ever be disappointed. The things you think when you're a kid can be funny. She wouldn't have been disappointed. She would have changed the color for me, I was sure.

The dresser still had my silver hairbrush sitting on it in front of the vanity mirror that was attached to it.

I ran my fingers over the white dresser remembering all the times Mother would reprimand me for not taking better care of my hair and smiled. It was amazing to have my memories back and not always be thinking that I was unwanted and thrown out on the streets.

I set the brush back on the dresser and it thumped against the wood. I froze.

"I heard something." A man's voice startled me. I jumped back from the dresser and raced to the door.

"You think it's the princess?" another man asked, excited.

"Princess, it's okay. We want to help you. The king's looking for you," the other man said while the first one snickered.

I rolled my eyes. *They have to know I'm not that dumb.*

I crept back into the passage and closed the door as quietly as I could manage, but the footsteps stopped and a door opened.

"I swear I heard something in here," the first voice said.

"It might have been a rodent or something."

"Rodents can open and close doors now, asshole?" the first man scoffed.

"C'mon, we need to find the princess before the High Councilor throws us in that human prison they're locking everyone up in."

They locked everyone up in a human prison? What the hell are they doing with the humans?

The door closed and footsteps faded down the hall. I

breathed a sigh of relief and slumped back against the cold stone wall.

Am I looking all over this place for nothing? Maybe I would have better luck finding help in the village.

There was little hope of finding survivors in the castle. Why hadn't I just run to the village and asked for someone to sift me back? That would have been equally as dangerous with Ronaldo having eyes and ears everywhere.

I followed the passageways through the castle to the kitchens, and what was normally a bustling kitchen with staff everywhere was cold and silent. He'd even got rid of the kitchen staff. What was his play here?

Was he planning to take over the castle, or give it to one of his cronies after he locked my father away?

It didn't matter one way or another, I was going to be stuck in this realm until I could find someone to help me, so I needed food.

Pots and pans hung from hooks around the marble island that still had a dusting of flour on it as if they were told to leave in the middle of cooking and they ran away.

I crept into the pantry where they kept the fruits and vegetables and found several small canvas bags that they used to take to market.

Grabbing two of the bags out of the pantry, I filled one with what I thought I would need in case I didn't get out of that mess soon, and the other I placed the book gently inside. At least that got it out of the back of my pants. I needed that book so I couldn't bear it if I dropped it and lost it.

It would mean the end of everything. Grey would be stuck

in the human world forever. I couldn't take that. It would break me.

"She must be here somewhere," someone said, walking into the kitchen.

I backed up into the pantry against the far wall, feeling for the lever I knew was there.

"What if she's not? What if she went back to the human world after the Shifter King and the High Councilor had us wasting our time searching for her?" another voice asked.

"It's not our job to ask questions. You know what happens when you question him."

Finally, I grasped the lever and pulled it. The back wall swung me in a circle and deposited me in the hidden room behind the pantry. It was sort of a secret panic room the kitchen staff would use if the castle was ever under attack.

Why hadn't they used it? Or did they? There was a tunnel in there that led to the castle grounds. They could have made a run for it.

"Did you hear that?" the voice said from the other side.

"Yeah, it sounded like gears grinding from the pantry."

Shit. I need to get out of here before they figure out there's a safe room back here.

On silent feet I raced down the passage until I hit a fork. One way would take me out of the castle but on the opposite side from where the village was, and it would be harder to get to the village without being spotted.

The other would take me back through the castle. Neither were great options, but I had a better chance of hiding inside the castle than I did outside.

I took the left-hand side and stayed in the castle. There were a few others who would know of the passageways, but not many. Could one of them be hiding too? It was a long shot but one I needed to take.

If someone else was hurt by the Council and I could have prevented it, I would never forgive myself.

I made it to the library and slipped inside. The space was exactly as I remembered it, shelves as tall as the ceiling and shorter shelves in neat rows throughout the massive space.

"I want her found!" Ronaldo roared as he slammed open the door. "Search for the castle's passageways and find her."

I scampered back behind a shelf to hide and waited for them to leave. I couldn't risk going back into the passageway with Ronaldo so close.

He may have been a scummy, oily bastard, but he wasn't dumb.

"Some of us have heard odd sounds like grinding gears or metal on stone. That might be her entering those passageways," the man from the kitchen said.

"And you didn't think to look for a secret exit? This is a castle. They have those kinds of protections built into them. Idiots."

"We did look, sir. There was nothing out of the ordinary in the girl's room or the kitchens," the man said.

"You didn't look hard enough, obviously. They're hidden for a reason." Ronaldo slammed his hand on one of the tables with a loud thwack that vibrated in my ears even from the distance I was from him.

This isn't good at all. He could find me here any second. I need to think. How do I get out of this without him finding the passages?

"Sir, we will find the girl. We will scour the entire castle for passages."

"Start in the library. There are always passages leading into the library." Ronaldo waved a hand.

Shit. Fuck. Shit.

I widened my eyes as two men went over to the shelves and started pulling books off. They threw them on the ground when they weren't what they were looking for.

I wracked my brain for anything that I could do to stop them from finding me once I closed the hidden door but came up empty.

My magic tingled beneath my skin, giving me an idea just as a man turned a corner and spotted me. *Shit.*

"Were you spying on us, Princess?" the man asked loudly.

"I don't know what you're talking about."

I slowly backed through the still open door to the passage. I needed to swing it closed but the man was still advancing on me.

Shadows appeared, writhing on my skin, and I thrust my hand out. The magic shoved him back enough that I slammed the door in his face.

My hands pulsed with energy as I laid them on the door, sealing it against everyone but me.

I needed to get out of there. Ronaldo would know soon enough that I had been spotted and they would be combing the entire castle looking for me. I jumped, startled as a deafening boom sounded from the other side.

He was destroying the library to get to me. That monster was hurting books so that he could capture and torture me again before killing me for the world to see.

Another boom rattled the stone walls and pieces of rock and dust from the ceiling rained down on me.

I backed up before turning left and right. Which way should I go? Back the way I came, or further down the passage?

More debris rained down on me, and I turned to the left. I needed to go further. They would probably be searching the kitchens next, looking for me since they'd spotted me in the library.

I sprinted down the passage until I was sure I was in a completely different wing of the castle and stopped to catch my breath, unused to this much running.

I rested my hands on the walls searching for the button I knew to be hidden there. It was the exact same stone as the rest of the wall and there were no seams or anything to even make someone think it was a possible exit.

My heartbeat quickened and my breathing became ragged when an arm wrapped around my middle and a hand covered my mouth. Whoever the man was, he tugged my back to his chest.

"Do not scream," he whispered.

I kicked my leg back trying to get him to loosen his hold. He grunted but only held me tighter.

"Stop." He shook me.

I opened my mouth to bite him because there was no way I was going to scream and alert Ronaldo to where I'd escaped to.

"Fuck, you play dirty." He grunted.

The man yanked me back into a different passageway all while keeping his hand over my mouth. Where was this man taking me?

I dug my heels into the ground, but he lifted me easily and dragged me down the dark passage.

What the hell do I do now? What does this guy plan to do to me? He wouldn't have cared if I screamed if he was one of Ronaldo's goons, so who is he and what is he doing in the castle?

An even better question, will I live long enough to get those answers?

CHAPTER 4

GREY

They led us into the prison with guns at our backs instead of the swords they had before. Electronic doors buzzed before swinging open for us, and I was shoved roughly inside.

"What the hell are we doing in a human prison?" I asked.

The guard at my back shoved me against the wall. "I said, no talking, mongrel."

"I'll show you a fucking mongrel." I bit out.

He dug his gun into my temple, but another guard stepped up and pulled it away. "The High Councilor wants this one alive."

"He's got a smart fucking mouth for someone in magic-blocking cuffs." The guard shoved me again, smacking my face into the wall.

"You can rough him up if he doesn't follow the rules or throw him in the hole, but you're not to kill him!" the new guard barked.

Each guard grabbed one of my arms and led me further into the prison. There were several levels in the inmate area.

"Are you okay?" Fenrick whispered so low I almost didn't hear him.

I nodded almost imperceptibly so I didn't piss off the guard who clearly wanted me dead. We needed to use this opportunity to figure out what was happening with the supernaturals and find a way to escape.

The guard shoved me to the left as the others were escorted elsewhere. I stopped digging in my heels as two men grabbed my arms and pulled me forward. I yanked my arm free of one of the guards.

We couldn't let them separate us. That would be the worst-case scenario in this place. How would we get out if we weren't together?

I spun around on the other guard and kicked him in the gut. The guard bent over with a groan, but the other guard recovered first and tackled me to the ground. My head hit the concrete, bounced off, and stars twinkled behind my eyes.

"Where are you taking him?" Fenrick bellowed.

The guard leading him sneered. "You should worry about your own life, traitor."

As soon as the other guard recovered, they pulled me to my feet. I shook my head to clear it and continued my struggle. The guard who stopped the other from killing me only minutes ago squeezed my arm and I glared back in defiance.

Wait. Did he just shake his head at me? It was so minute I almost think I imagined it.

"Where are you taking me?" I struggled to get free again even though it was futile.

The Shadow King tried to get to me but the guard at his back pulled him away as he yanked at his arms. "That's my daughter's mate. You will not separate us."

"You don't make the rules here, *King*." The guard at his back sneered.

Fenrick pulled out of his guard's hold and launched himself toward me before one of the guards pointed his gun at Fenrick's head. Fenrick stopped and stood deadly still.

"There are no orders to keep the rest of you alive," the guard who saved me earlier said. "I would be very careful in your choices."

I wrenched my arm from his grasp, ready to knock the gun away with everything I had. Those were *my* people, and I would do anything to keep them safe.

"No!" Magna screamed. "Don't resist, Grey."

I glanced at her and the terror on her face was real. Something terrible was going to happen if this continued. Sometimes Magna saw too much.

I scanned the faces of the others noting their deadly stillness. This definitely wouldn't end well. The guard cocked his weapon as Fenrick stared him down.

I nodded my understanding and relaxed my shoulders. I wouldn't struggle again. No matter what. I trusted Magna's visions.

"Stand down, Fenrick," I said, eyeing the Fae who'd become a friend. "There will be no death today. Don't give them what they want."

"But..." Fenrick sighed and took a step back.

The guard disarmed his weapon and grabbed me roughly around the biceps again.

"Fine. Take me to whatever fresh hell you have planned for me." I let them yank me down the hall.

"You're going to wish you'd struggled harder, Shifter King." The guard to my left chuckled.

"You're all going to wish you picked the winning side when I come for you in the end." I couldn't help the words that rolled off my tongue.

They weren't a threat, they were a promise. One way or another, I was going to end all the traitors to the crown.

"You keep saying that, but look where you are, and I don't think you will have such a cocky attitude after your session." He shoved me forward.

The halls were long painted a drab gray, probably meant to destroy all hope in the inmates there. Cells lined the walls and people stared out the little plexiglass windows at me as I was shoved past them.

An electronic buzzing met my ears as we got to another door that needed a keycard to enter. The guard on my right flashed his badge over the scanner and the click was ominous. I didn't want to go in that place but what choice did I have?

If I fought them, I would probably die or worse. There was no escaping it, so I just had to accept it.

They walked me through what appeared to be a medical unit, but everything was wrong. The sterile scent of rubbing alcohol was in the air but there were people hooked up to machines and people in white lab coats poking and prodding them.

The people struggled against their bonds as they were strapped down and gagged. They weren't on those beds willingly. They were being tested on like lab rats. It was the very reason we'd always protected our secrets, and now it was our own kind doing it to each other.

What the fuck?

I was dragged into a room with a bed that was similar to those in the hall and braced myself for whatever testing they were going to do to me. They strapped me down, the cuffs still hindering any use of magic.

When they were finished, Ronaldo stepped in the room. A hint of madness glinted in his eyes as he smiled gleefully at me. "You will tell me all your secrets."

"The fuck I will."

This isn't about experimenting on me. This is a torture session. Just great.

"How the hell am I gonna be your slave if I'm being tortured?" I scoffed.

"You'll heal." He picked up a scalpel and ripped through my shirt, nicking the skin in several places, but I didn't flinch. "Tell me where the princess is."

"Go to hell," I said through gritted teeth.

He jabbed me with the tip of the scalpel and blood squirted from the wound in my chest. Pain seared me like fire, but I still refused to react.

That was what he wanted. He fed on people's screams. I would die on that table before I ever gave in and screamed for him.

When he stabbed me again on the other side of my chest and blood spurted everywhere but I still didn't flinch or react, he started getting frustrated. His brows pinched in anger as he sliced through my skin.

I may just die on this table.

My wolf howled in my mind, taking most of the pain from me so I could hold my ground, but I knew it wouldn't last long with Ronaldo hacking away at me.

"It can all stop if you tell me where the princess is hiding," Ronaldo purred.

"Fuck you."

"Give me the little hammer." Ronaldo waved to the guard.

The guard handed him a small surgical hammer. I didn't need to be told what that was for, it was for breaking bones.

Not sure how long I will last without screaming if he does what I think he's about to.

"I'm going to break all the bones in your hand one by one until you tell me where the princess is." Ronaldo grinned.

I balled my hands into fists, but the guard gripped my wrist, hitting the one pressure point in it that made my fist open on reflex. Ronaldo gripped my pinky finger with one hand and lifted the hammer over his head before slamming it down on the second knuckle.

My back arched as blinding pain tore through my hand, but I didn't make a sound. Still, I reacted though, and that was enough motivation for the sadist to continue his torture.

"Don't want to tell me where the princess is then we can change the topic of conversation," Ronaldo said. "Where is your facility? I know you have people. Where are they?"

"I'm not telling you anything. Break the bones in my hands. Before the end of this, I will see you dead."

"Wrong answer." Ronaldo grinned before slamming the hammer down on my ring finger.

I panted through the pain, not willing to give in and scream. He broke three more knuckles before he grabbed the scalpel again and dug it into my left pec. I couldn't see what he was doing but the cuts and pain were in a pattern along my skin.

Blood dripped down my side, sliding along my skin. I clenched my good hand into a fist my nails bit into my palm, that little bite of pain taking some of the pain in the other hand and making it manageable.

"You're wasting your time. I told you I won't tell you anything."

"You misunderstand what this is, Shifter King," Ronaldo spit the word *king* at me. "This is fun for me."

I already knew that, but the evil grin on his face was slightly terrifying. He got high on causing pain.

How much does he enjoy the suffering of those people he's experimenting on? Do I really want to know?

"You can stop the pain and ruin my fun if you just answer my questions, mutt."

Blood ran rivers down my sides as he continued to carve something into my chest. I squeezed my eyes closed and panted through gritted teeth.

I will not break. I will not break.

My people and Aurelia meant more to me than my own life. I would never tell this monster where to find them. "Do what you want to me. I won't tell you shit."

"I hope you enjoy the marks permanently in your skin then." Ronaldo sat back and admired whatever the hell he'd done to my chest. "Without your magic, this will scar before it gets the chance to heal."

He grabbed a mirror and pointed at an angle so I could see my chest. I shouldn't have looked. I knew I should have kept my eyes closed but curiosity got the better of me and I glanced at the mirror. *Shifter scum* was etched into my chest in blocky handwriting.

I'm going to destroy this motherfucker.

Ronaldo's laugh grated on me as he picked up the hammer once more. I wasn't going to make it out of this unscathed, so it didn't matter what he carved into my skin.

I closed my eyes once more and waited for the pain. The anticipation was almost worse than the pain itself. I had to relax my muscles and breathe through my nose so I didn't make it worse.

If I tense up waiting for it to happen it would only be worse. Its why people in car accidents who see it coming and tense up always are the worst injured.

I nearly screamed as my thumb caught fire and white spots danced behind my closed lids. A grunt of pain escaped and my back arched off the bed as the blinding pain tore through my hand and traveled up my arm to my elbow.

"Tell me where she is!" Ronaldo screamed.

Without warning or waiting for my answer, he slammed the hammer down again and again until I lost the battle and bellowed my agony.

Shame didn't get a chance to take root inside me as Ronaldo laughed and slammed the hammer down again. Black overtook all my senses as I passed out from pain and blood loss.

CHAPTER 5

AURELIA

My scream was muffled by his hand as he took me through a passage into a dark room.

Could I have been wrong about him not being a part of the Council's guards? I thrashed against him, and the kiss of metal armor met my skin.

If he wasn't with the Council, why was he wearing armor? My father's army was rounded up by the Council and their minions.

How likely was it that this man who was abducting me was able to escape the Council on his own? But then why did he keep me quiet and take me to a dark room?

"Shut up, Princess," his gravelly voice whispered next to my ear. "I'm going to remove my hand. If you scream, we are both completely fucked."

There was my answer. He either pretended to join the Council to find me himself, or he was able to hide without them catching him.

I didn't have any choice but to listen to him when he put it like that. Screaming was a terrible idea when the Council had men all over the castle searching for me but still, could I trust a stranger in the middle of the lion's den?

No. But maybe we could help each other if he answered my questions.

I nodded my head in understanding and he released me. "Who are you?"

I glanced at the armor he was wearing and recognized it as the armor my father's army wore, but I had never seen him before. Not even in the childhood memories that were recently restored.

"My name is Kiernan, and I was in your father's militia. His elite force that was sent to find you when you were abducted from your bed."

"Then why weren't you there when Fenrick found me at the portal? I don't remember seeing you there." I crossed my arms over my chest and allowed my magic to pool in my palms.

"I was in the human world pretending to be a warlock and looking for you, Princess." He bowed his head.

"Why have I never seen you before, and how did you escape the Council? How do I know you're not a spy?" I asked the questions rapid fire.

"Whoa, Princess. Take it easy on the questions. I'll answer, but you need to breathe." He raised his hands in surrender.

I arched a brow at him, waiting for an answer, magic at the ready in case he wasn't who he said.

"The Council came in unexpectedly not long after you and your parents escaped from their fucked-up meeting." He ran a hand over his head. "I had just been called back because you had resurfaced, and I was in the castle. They didn't know I was even here."

"How long have you been hiding?" I asked, but he held up a finger.

"They attacked the barracks first and had men on the inside. They brought everyone to the courtyard, and I watched from that window as they gave them a choice. They either swore allegiance to the Council or they were sent to the dungeons."

His eyes were haunted before he squeezed them tightly and blew out a resigned breath. "I need to find a way to get them out of the dungeon so we can take back our kingdom and stop their evil plans of world domination."

"There's no one in the dungeons," I whispered.

"What?" His eyes narrowed on mine.

"My father and my mate, along with Fenrick and a friend were arrested by the Council. They're still searching for me. I went to the dungeons first to release my father's men that were still loyal to him, but the dungeons are empty." I flopped into a wingback armchair.

"They're not there? Where are they?" He planted his hands on his hips and paced.

"I don't know. I wish I did, because that was my only hope of saving my father and mate." I tilted my head back and blinked away the tears of hopelessness forming in my eyes.

"Do you know where the king was taken?" he asked.

"No. I think they were taken back to the human realm, but I'm not certain." I clenched my fists at my sides, still unsure if I could trust this Fae.

He said he was militia but didn't say why I'd never seen him before and completely ignored my spy question.

"Why would the Council take them to the human realm? They hate it there." Kiernan rubbed his chin.

"They have some kind of deal with the humans, we think. We were outed to the humans because they have some kind of chemical that makes shifters go into a rage and shift randomly. It was caught on camera."

"Shit," Kiernan said.

"Yeah, it's pretty bad and I need an army, but I can't even sift back to the human realm to get help. I've been wandering around the castle but every second I stay here is one second closer to them catching me and doing gods know what to me."

"You can't sift?" he asked, and I glared at him. "That's right, you're a young one."

"Yes, but I'm not dumb or naïve. How do I know you're not a spy for the Council just trying to gain my trust and any information I have before you turn me over to them?"

"You don't. And you're smart for not trusting me just because I wear your father's armor. Some of those men were right there with the Council guards rounding everyone up."

"Fair enough." I nodded.

"I wouldn't trust anyone, especially those who tell you to trust them. They are the worst." He flexed a hand at his side.

"What are we going to do, then?" I asked, ignoring the jaded comment from the man.

"I don't know. What was your reason for wandering around the castle?"

"Trying to find someone to sift me back to the human world and not get caught by Ronaldo and his guards." I sighed.

"Why the human world?" he asked frowning.

"We have a sizable army there that can help us, and I'm the

only one that can get them back into Faery." I chewed my lip nervously.

"Then let's go get your army." He held out a hand to me but I hesitated, still not sure I could trust him.

What if he was a spy looking for the location of the facility and Grey's people? Could I lead him to our army and ruin everything?

"I can see the indecision in your eyes. You don't trust me." He nodded like that was to be expected.

"This whole *nice guy here to save the day* thing could be an act to get me to tell you where the facility is so the Council can attack." I raised a brow at him.

"Good girl," he said before dropping to one knee and resting his sword on his hands.

"What are you doing?" I gasped.

"I swear to the gods and on my honor to protect and serve Princess Aurelia of the Shadow Kingdom until my dying breath." Kiernan bowed his head.

Magic tingled in the air, wrapping around me and squeezing my chest. He'd just made a magical vow to serve and protect me.

I did not see that coming.

"Well, that was unexpected."

"I won't tell you pretty lies but will give you the truth, always, Princess. I won't tell you that you can trust me but prove myself the best way that I can. With my vow."

"What about your vow to my father?" I asked, wide-eyed.

"It's because of my vow to your father that I made this vow to you. He would want someone to be on your side while he can't be here."

He was still kneeling on the ground, and I had a feeling he would remain there until I told him to move.

"Okay, you proved your point. You can get up now." I waved a hand for him to move.

"If people bowing to you makes you uncomfortable, you are going to have a very hard time being the princess you were born to be," Kiernan said with a chuckle as he got to his feet once more.

"I get that, but the whole vow to protect and serve me was what made me slightly uncomfortable." I stood from the chair.

"Fair enough."

I blew out a relieved breath and my shoulders slumped.

What are we going to do now? I have a guard from my father's militia sworn to me and we are still behind enemy lines.

"Would you be comfortable taking me to this army of yours, now?" Kiernan asked.

"It's not so much of an army in the traditional sense but they will fight for Grey and to get back into Faery." I adjusted the bags on my shoulder.

The book heated through the canvas, comforting me that it was still in my possession. I needed it more than almost anything. There was something in it that could help us with the Council. There had to be. I just needed time to find it.

"Can they fight in a battle or are they civilians?" he asked.

"They are basically mercenaries."

It was the only way I could describe the people at Grey's building. They got in a ring to decide disputes. It was a bit barbaric, but I hadn't seen one since Layla tried to drag me into a fight.

"Mercenaries?" he scoffed. "Why would a princess work with a group of criminals?"

"I didn't always know I was a princess." I planted my hands on my hips, glaring at him.

He didn't have the right to judge me or the people at the Syndicate. They may not have liked me all that much in the beginning, but they would do what they needed when the time came.

"Right, sorry, Princess. I forgot." He bowed his head.

"It's fine. Just don't judge them. They've been looked down on by the Fae their entire lives and won't take kindly to it from you when we go back there without Grey."

"Understood. Now, how do we get to this place?" he asked.

"We will need to sift."

That was going to be the hard part of all of this. I needed to trust him enough to put the image in his mind.

"That's going to be a problem. The castle is warded against sifting in or out." Kiernan ran a hand down his face.

"Fuck." I practically yelled.

Kiernan flinched and scanned the room for any threats. *Shit. I forgot we were being hunted. Good job, Aurelia.*

"I know a place in the woods that we can sift from without anyone seeing us."

"Yeah, the problem with that is getting there without being seen," I huffed.

"I guess you don't know all the passages in this place then, do you, Princess?" Kiernan grinned.

He turned to the passageway he'd dragged me through only moments ago and we hurried through the tunnels to a part of the castle I'd never been to.

"There are passages that lead to the barracks?" I asked in a whisper.

"In case of emergency we can get to the king faster. A few of the king's most trusted soldiers knew of them."

"That's actually pretty smart." I nodded.

We crept along silently until light filtered in below a door that I'd never seen before. Kiernan tapped on something, and stone ground against metal. I flinched at the loud sound and held my breath until the door swung completely open.

We were in the woods. The tall trees towered over us as we rushed from the passage. There were shrubs and tall grass darting the area, and when I spun around, I found we'd just walked out of a small cabin.

Kiernan grabbed my hand, and I gave him the image in my mind. We spun through time and space before my feet landed on soft grass right outside the wards.

"Let me do the talking. They can be temperamental," I said and crossed the wards.

"Stop!" someone yelled, and guns were immediately pointed at my face.

I put my hands up in the air. "It's me. Grey's in trouble and we need your help."

A man I'd never seen before stepped forward. "Grey's not here. Now I'm in charge. Make one false move and I'll shoot, princess or not."

Who is that? Has the Council taken over here too? We are royally screwed if they did. I just walked to my own death.

CHAPTER 6

GREY

"What happened?" Fenrick yelled.

I blinked my eyes open, barely able to see the blurry outline of the Fae guardian who had quickly become a friend.

"Watch it, traitor," The guard carrying me snapped and dropped me on the cold concrete.

I gasped as pain burned my back. The joints popped as I crashed to the floor.

The guard stomped from the cell but the other watched us closely.

"I'll be back later," the guard whispered and closed the cell.

Why did he whisper? Is he on our side?

I groaned, my head fuzzy. I blinked my eyes closed and willed the room to stop spinning.

"What is that on your chest?" Fenrick gasped.

"Ronaldo's parting gift." I coughed and curled in on myself.

It wasn't that I didn't want Fenrick to see it. I didn't

care if he did. But I needed to protect myself and my body instinctively curled so my wounds weren't on display.

"I can't heal you with the cuffs on," Fenrick said regret filling his tone.

"It's okay, I can't shift to heal either." I shook my head and winced when pain sliced through it.

Did they kick my ass once I passed out? Why does my head hurt so badly? I don't remember Ronaldo punching me in the head.

"They did a number on you and wanted you to suffer. How are we going to mix with the rest of the population when you can't even stand?" Fenrick sighed.

"Maybe that's the point. He wants to torture me and then starve me because I can't move." I moaned as I tried and failed to sit up.

"That guard whispered he would be back. He's the same one who stopped the guy from shooting you. Do you think he meant he would come back to help?" Fenrick asked thoughtfully.

"We can't trust anyone here, Fenrick. They are all from the Council. They are the enemy," I said, gritting my teeth against the throbbing pain in my hand.

"But he didn't seem to want you dead. His expression when the guard dumped you on the ground was murderous for a second before it went completely blank."

My oversensitive hearing picked up boots stomping down the hall outside our cell and I shushed Fenrick before the door opened again. That same guard came through and closed the door behind him.

He crouched in front of me with wide eyes. "I can't fully heal you or they will know someone on staff helped you."

"Why are you helping?" I gritted out.

"Dan sent me. He knew something major was going on when you all took so long to come back to the Syndicate." He placed a hand over mine and green healing magic spread through me, popping my bones back into place.

I nearly screamed at the pain but locked my jaw so I couldn't open my mouth and alert anyone.

"What are you doing?" Fenrick stomped up to the man.

"I'm healing his crushed fingers. They used a hammer and broke his bones," the guard said. "You can heal. You know how painful that can be for a patient."

He moved his hand when relief flooded me, and I flexed my still stiff hand.

"How are you able to heal?" I asked.

"I'm half Fae. It was the only way I could be a guard in here." The man moved his hand over my chest.

"So, basically the half Fae children they abandoned to a cold new reality are welcomed back as long as they do their dirty work. Got it." I shook my head.

Ronaldo was a piece of shit. I would be dealing with him soon. Just as soon as I got out of this hellhole.

"Basically, but it's good for us because now I can get word to Dan about where you are, and they can get a team here." The guard pulled his hand from my chest with a look of apology.

"I get it. Your life is on the line if they find out you healed me. I'll survive. Thank you." I dipped my head to the man and sat up.

I was still stiff, and pinpricks of pain hit me as I moved a certain way, but I could at least move. Ronaldo would be pissed I could, though. I grinned at the thought of the man being angry because I healed fast.

Every little win counted against that man, even if I was being petty.

"I have to go, but I'll help if I can." the guard whispered and left the room.

I glanced at Fenrick with a raised brow, wondering how in the hell that just happened. "Did that really just happen?"

"It did. How on earth did Dan get a plant in here so quickly?" Fenrick shook his head.

"Dan is really fucking resourceful. He also knows just about everyone in the supernatural community in Dallas. He always gets the job done."

Could I hope that Dan had a way to get us out of here? Every guard I'd seen so far appeared to be Fae. What happened to the human guards who worked here before?

"Well, despite what he did to Aurelia, I'm glad he's on our side." Fenrick held out a hand to help me up.

"Same. He didn't really mean for all of that to happen, though. I punished him for what went down." I grabbed a shirt from the bottom bunk and pulled it over my head.

The marks weren't entirely healed, and I didn't want everyone to see that I'd been marked. I flexed my hand and winced when it was still a bit sore.

The guard had been right. If Ronaldo found out that I healed completely already there would be an investigation and we would lose the advantage. It was a great turn of events to have a guard on our side.

An electronic buzzing sound filled the room and the door swung open. I glanced at Fenrick, who shrugged.

"They do that when it's time to go to the mess hall." He stepped out of the cell into the throng of people rushing from their cells.

"How long did he have me chained to a table?" I asked.

"I've been here for three solid meals already so I'm guessing a full day." He nudged me when I stopped walking.

Shit. No wonder my head is fuzzy.

"Okay, then show me the way." My stomach took that moment to growl.

When I'd been in pain I hadn't realized how hungry I was but with the mention of food, my stomach rumbled in protest. Even my wolf whimpered in my mind, starving as well.

I followed Fenrick down the maze of cells to a large room. There were no windows and a buffet-style line sat in the corner. There were human guards mixed with the Fae guards. I raised an eyebrow at Fenrick, but he shrugged.

"They have some kind of arrangement," he whispered as he handed me a tray.

There were workers behind plexiglass dishing out some kind of disgusting looking slop. My wolf whined his agreement about whatever the hell it was they were feeding us as we moved down the line.

"We already guessed that, but the humans look uncomfortable being in the same room with the Fae," I said scanning the guards.

I pitched forward as I was shouldered in the back. I nearly busted my face on the plexiglass but caught myself. I spun to find the man striding away.

What the fuck was that about?

I turned back and retrieved my tray and food as Fenrick marched over to a table in the corner. Relief flooded me as I spotted two familiar faces at the table. The Shadow King nodded as I sat across from him and Magna smiled.

"You didn't struggle," she said with what sounded like relief.

"No, I let him carve those awful words into my chest and break my hand," I growled.

Magna winced, tears filling her eyes, but I shook my head. I didn't need tears. I needed revenge and a way out of this fucking cesspool.

"Sorry," I said after a moment. "Sometimes I forget that you see too much."

I set my tray down on the table and picked up the fork to take a bite of whatever the gruel was when I noticed the separation of the guards.

The human guards were clearly confused about what was happening and why. They whispered to each other, probably unaware that the Fae guards could hear them.

"The humans are scared and confused," I whispered, leaning into the others. "We can probably use that to our advantage."

I put the spoon to my lips and grimaced. The slop didn't even smell appetizing in the slightest, but I still shoveled it into my mouth. I couldn't be picky when eating meant the difference between life and death.

"Look what we have here," a deep voice echoed through the now silent mess hall.

I turned to see a huge shifter that I'd never seen before

staring directly at me. He had to be some kind of bear and we never really got along with the bears.

"And what is that?" I asked, turning and standing at full height.

"The great Shifter King was caught by the Fae? Your father must be rolling over in his grave right now." The shifter laughed.

Wrong thing to say, asshole. He was the first but definitely wouldn't be the last to challenge me in this shithole. It was the way of the world in a prison like that. You always took out the biggest motherfucker first.

I could definitely handle that.

"What grave?" I asked. "He wasn't dead until a few weeks ago, and I doubt the *High Councilor* gave him the courtesy of a burial."

The shifter sneered, not caring at all that his barb didn't stick, or the information that my father had been alive or in prison for centuries bothered me.

"Hey!" a guard shouted. "Do we have a problem here?"

I lifted a brow at the shifter in question. "I don't know. I don't have a problem, but he clearly does."

The shifter's face turned red as he took a threatening step forward. "You have a big mouth. Someone should do something about that."

The shifter balled his fist, and I felt more than heard the chairs screeching across the tile behind me. I waved Fenrick and the Shadow King off, not wanting them to get into trouble with me as I stared down the bully in front of me.

"You gonna do something about it?" I taunted, and the shifter swung a meaty fist at my head.

I ducked and the shifter spun around. I kicked out a leg and sent him to the ground in a heap. He hit his head on a nearby table and bumped into a warlock, who growled.

My movements were stiff as the warlock turned on me with a glare. I wasn't the one who bumped into him, but apparently everyone had a chip on his shoulder in this place.

Chaos ensued just as the warlock punched me in the face, turning everything black.

CHAPTER 7

AURELIA

"You're not in charge. Where's Dan?" I yelled as they surrounded us with guns drawn.

I didn't recognize a single one of them, but I hadn't met everyone in the Syndicate. I glared at the man in front of me. Was he part of the Council? Could they have broken Grey's wards and taken over the place?

No. I felt Grey's wards as we stepped over them. This was something different. Idiots on a power trip maybe?

Either way, this was bad. How was I going to get their help if they locked us in a cell? A gun dug into my back as the shifter shoved me forward.

Where is everyone? Where are Dan and Asher? They would be able to tell these idiots to stop this.

"Dan is gone," a shifter whispered behind me.

I glanced over my shoulder at the woman her brows were pinched in confusion. She didn't hesitate to shove me forward though.

"Gone where? He's in charge here, not you," I growled.

I glanced at Kiernan. He had his sword in its scabbard but his hand was on the hilt just waiting for the opportunity to use it.

"Stop asking questions," the man said in a gruff tone. "You're the reason the boss left us, and I will see you punished for his disappearance, wicked Fae."

"It's always going to come back to that isn't it? It has nothing to do with Grey, but your own prejudice against the Fae. It was our Council. The same Council bastards we're fighting against." I threw my hands up.

The action sent everyone into motion, cocking their guns, ready to take me out.

"I have no problem shooting you, Princess." The man got right up in my face with a sneer. "Come with us quietly and you won't become a stain on the concrete."

"Where are the riders of the hunt?" I demanded. "Dan should have left one of them in charge. This is ridiculous."

They didn't answer my question, instead prodding me in the back to move. Kiernan placed a hand on my shoulder and squeezed it in support.

"They won't kill you, Princess. I won't allow it," Kiernan whispered.

I nodded. Our magic could probably be faster than bullets. Maybe. Kiernan would know better than me, but it wasn't something I could ask him at the moment. I really didn't want to test that theory.

They steered us to the parking garage, and I groaned, hoping I didn't get thrown in a cell next to that crazy bitch who screamed all the time. Wouldn't that just be poetic justice?

I turned to peer at Kiernan, wondering what he was thinking about all this as Asher burst from the elevator.

"What the fuck are you morons doing?" Asher bellowed as he stomped toward us.

His face red with his rage, the guards' deaths shown in his eyes. Finally, someone who could talk sense to these people.

"The Fae are a problem," the man who claimed to be in charge said. "They cannot be trusted."

"Grey will do worse to you then he did to that backstabbing bitch if you don't let his mate go. Do you have any idea who she is?" Asher asked, getting in the shifter's face.

"Yes, I know she is the reason Grey is gone and she is the reason the Council is murderous. She is the reason they are taking over the world and rounding us up like dogs!" the shifter yelled.

"Excuse me?" I screeched. "What is this about the Council rounding everyone up?"

"Don't talk to me, Fae whore." The man sneered.

Asher took a swing at the guy the same time Kiernan pulled his sword. The man was thrown to the ground by Asher's punch and Kiernan nicked the man's throat with his blade as Kiernan tilted the shifter's chin up.

"You ever speak to the future queen of Faery that way again and banishment will look like a walk in the park," Kiernan said with a deadly calm.

Asher clenched his fists at his sides, ready for the shifter to argue so he could lay him out again.

I shook my head. "I've finally figured out a way for us all to go home and this is the reception I get."

The rest of the riders of the hunt blocked the elevator doors and Zeke winked at me. They were intimidating, but I was tired of being protected by intimidating men.

"Home to Faery?" someone whispered.

I ignored it.

"It doesn't matter what she says!" the shifter on his knees bellowed. "She's the reason the boss is gone, and she should be punished."

"The boss is gone because he was helping me find what we need to send everyone home to Faery!" I shouted.

I was so done with this bullshit.

Asher stomped forward, picking the shifter up off the concrete. "She is your boss' mate and deserves the same respect you showed him."

"It's okay, Asher. Grey rules with fear so maybe I should have started with that." I let my hands glow with my magic and stepped around the man next to Asher.

The rest of the guards shifted nervously from foot to foot, fidgeting with the safety mechanisms on their guns, most likely unsure of what they should be doing.

Shadows pulsed up my arms, and the man gulped. His pulse fluttered erratically, fear thick in his eyes. "I'm in charge while Dan is gone."

"You will never be in charge!" Asher roared.

He shook the man violently. The rest of his brothers created an imposing wall of pissed-off riders of the hunt in front of the elevator.

"Put your guns down," Zeke said, his tone lethal.

What could the riders of the hunt have done that scared everyone so much? Ever since they helped Grey rescue me from Malcolm, they had been nothing but kind and respectful to me.

Seeing the murderous side of them was different, and I was glad they were on my side.

The group surrounding us glanced between each other and the man who was leading them and then finally holstered their weapons.

"Now, move." Asher dropped the man to the concrete and shoved past several of the guards circling me.

The guards scattered, and I glanced up at Asher's murderous expression. He was a big softy when he wanted to be, but he could scare the life out of someone as well.

"Asher, it's fine." I sighed, letting the magic drop.

"C'mon, Princess. We need to know what's happening. Your mother is beside herself with worry." Asher wrapped an arm around my shoulders.

"What about him?" someone shouted behind me. "He could be a spy."

"He's with me. He saved me and swore a magical vow. No one touch him." I spun on the group still surrounding Kiernan.

"You heard the princess, now move." Asher took a threatening step toward the group, and they all backed away from Kiernan, hands up in surrender.

"That's a neat trick." Kiernan smirked.

"These idiots piss me off. I don't usually throw my weight around like that, but with Grey and Dan both gone, it's getting a bit ridiculous around here." Asher shook his head as he led me to the elevators.

Zeke nodded his head as he stepped out of the way. "Glad to see you're safe, Princess. We were worried about you."

"I was worried there for a bit myself." I chuckled.

Kiernan jogged up next to me. "Did you say the queen is here?"

"Yes, she's here and more than a little worried about her family disappearing," Ash said, shooting me a pointed look.

"Later. I don't want everyone to hear this." I glanced around the parking garage warily.

I stepped inside the elevator, and the riders along with Kiernan all followed me inside. Asher hit the button for the top floor, and we rode up in silence.

I blew out a breath when we got to the top floor and grinned. This place felt like home. I was so glad to be back here. I rushed down the hall to Grey's office and forgot for a second that he wasn't there when the office smelled like him.

I spun around in a circle just breathing it in for a second before seeing Asher with a look of amusement.

"Did you miss this place?" Ash asked, chuckling.

I shrugged. "I did. It's a thousand times better than hiding in the dusty passageways of the castle and running from Ronaldo's guards."

"Fair enough." Ash bowed his head to me.

"How long has Dan been gone?" I asked.

I sat down in Grey's chair behind his desk, glancing between the riders of the hunt. They were all huge, imposing figures, though I'd only got to know Asher and Zeke.

"He's been gone a couple days. We aren't sure what he's plotting." Asher ran a hand down his face.

"Grey and my father along with Fenrick and Magna have been captured by the Council." I dropped the bomb no one wanted to hear.

"Fuck," Ash cursed.

"Yeah, my thoughts exactly. We need to find them because I have no idea how long they will let them live." I chewed my lip nervously.

"Do you know where they've taken him?" Ash asked.

His body was coiled tightly, and he kept clenching and unclenching his fists at his sides. I never asked how they knew each other or what kind of relationship the hunters had with my mate. There was never time.

"No. I'm guessing somewhere in the human realm, because they dragged them to the portal after they were captured."

It was the only thing that made sense, but at the same time, it didn't make sense. Why drag them to the portal instead of the Council chambers?

Zeke sat at the conference table and pulled out his laptop, searching for any clue as to what was going on and where Grey might have been taken.

"I think we need to talk to the shifter again. What jail was he in?" I asked.

There had been something very wrong with the place they had kept him. He should have been able to use his strength to get away, but he couldn't.

"I want a sample of whatever they dosed him with," Zeke said, never looking from his laptop.

"What good will that do?" I drummed my fingers on the desk.

"If we know what it is, we may be able to find a way to counter it. The shifter said it was chemical and felt like bottled rage. That's a terrifying combination when working with shifters." Zeke continued tapping on the keys.

Asher sat in the chair next to him with a huff. "We need to work on one thing at a time."

"Agreed. Kiernan," I pointed to the Fae. "Is there anything you remember from your time in the castle?"

"I heard many conversations about the human government, but you already seem to know that they are working together," Kiernan said.

"It's the only thing that makes sense. They used a chemical on the shifter so he would shift into his wolf on camera." I shook my head.

"That stunt caused a lot of civil unrest. Plus, there were fae guards in the human jail." Ash pointed out.

"We don't know how deep this alliance goes, though. Were those guards just planted there, or did the human government allow them to be brought in? How much do the people in the prisons know about what's happening there?"

"Those are all very good questions that we do not have the answers to." Ash slammed his fist on the table.

"We need to get them and soon. Every day that Grey is in their clutches could be his last." I laid my forehead on the desk and blew out a breath.

The Fates can't take him yet. He's mine and if I lose him, it will break me beyond repair.

CHAPTER 8

GREY

I screamed as something hit me in the back and electricity burned beneath my skin. My body twitched uncontrollably as I flopped on the ground like a fish.

Fuck. That hurt.

Hands gripped my arms, hauling me to my feet, but my knees buckled and I would have crashed to the ground again if the guards weren't holding me up.

"Picking fights in here is a very bad idea," the guard who helped me before whispered.

"I didn't pick that fight. He attacked me." I tried to shrug him off, but I was still sore from the torture session.

"It doesn't matter. That's not what the guards saw. You're going in the hole," he said so everyone heard.

That is not the place I want to be.

I glanced over my shoulder at the others' worried faces and winked, letting them know it would be okay. At least for now I wasn't going to get another torture session.

"Let this be a lesson, new people." The guard holding me up turned his glare on everyone in the room. "If you fight, you will get electrocuted and sent to the hole for a full day. If you do it again, it's a week."

He shoved me out the door for good measure. Everyone was watching, after all.

"You just made things exponentially more difficult." He whispered so low, only a shifter could hear.

"That wasn't my fault. I don't go around picking fights," I said.

He yanked on my arm to get me to move faster as he dragged me through the halls. Cells lined each wall, but there was no one inside them. Everyone was in the mess hall, eating garbage and probably gossiping about the fight.

"Some of the guards seem uncomfortable." I changed the subject.

"The humans are scared of us. They know they aren't strong enough to take us down without those batons. It's why they were given those when witches and shifters were brought in."

He was sharing information, but I had a feeling he would keep up the act no matter what went down. Even though he'd healed me, I couldn't trust the guy. If it came down to getting us out of here or his life, he would choose his life and I couldn't fault him for that.

He led me to a heavy metal door that had an ominous feel to it. I reared back, not liking the looks of this at all. He swiped his badge across the scanner and that electric buzzing echoed through the hall as the door slid open.

I understood now why they called it the hole. There were

no lights in the two-by-two cell. No windows let any light in either. I was going to be sitting in the dark for an entire day, completely alone.

Just fucking great.

"If this happens again, it's a week, Grey. You need to be careful in here," he whispered before closing the door and blocking out all light.

The box was so small I couldn't stretch my legs out when I sat down. Guards passed every so often, their words the only company I had.

"We're going to be getting even more of the crazies," a guard said. "They're rounding them all up."

What the fuck? They're really going that far?

I had thought the country was founded because of persecution, and now they were doing this just because they were scared?

"Not all of them are going to prison," another voice said. "They have special intake facilities to see if they're a threat to humanity."

I call bullshit. I doubt anyone comes out of those facilities alive. They are just saying that so they can have an excuse to test on my people. I need to get out of here. My people are in fucking danger, and I'm stuck in this fucking box.

"Do you really think they'll let any of them go? You're an idiot, if you do," the first guard scoffed. "They're too dangerous."

"Locking them all up forever doesn't make sense though, either. They're a drain on our resources locked in prisons and facilities."

"Are you becoming a bleeding heart, Thomas? You saw that

brawl in there. If they didn't have those cuffs on, it would have been a lot worse."

"I'm not a bleeding heart," Thomas grunted.

The hall went quiet after that, and I had no clue how long I'd been curled up on the floor of the tiny cell when more voices filtered in.

"I don't know why we have to listen to that guy," a new voice hit me from the hall.

"He's got an in with some high-profile people, including the Department of Justice," someone responded.

"So he can just take over? I had friends that were laid off so his freaks could come in and run the place."

"I would watch your tone, man. I get it. I do, but there's something seriously off about that guy. He has his own room in the medical unit, and people have heard screams coming from it," the new voice warned.

"You think he's torturing people? That's not even legal," the second voice huffed.

"Are they people, though? Do they get the same human rights we do when they aren't even human?"

"No, you're right. They aren't human, so the laws don't apply to them. That's why they can all be rounded up and dealt with. No activists will care that animals are being treated like animals."

I shifted in my position on the floor and clenched my hand into a fist. These assholes really wanted to be gutted by a wolf's claws. They were fucking begging for it.

I couldn't do that though. If I killed a human guard, the punishment would be far more severe than a day in the hole. I doubt Ronaldo would let the humans sentence me to death though. He wanted my death for himself.

"That's a pretty fucked-up view, man." The first guard chuckled.

"You saw the video of the guy who turned into a raging wolf. That's the shit we're dealing with in here. I do not get paid enough to have to worry about getting nailed by a fucking wolf."

"The President of the United States said Homeland Security is handling it," the first man said.

"Yeah, *handling it* means they become our problem."

Those assholes were seriously pissing me off. They had no care for the fact that despite us not being human, we were still intelligent people with families and innocent children. I tuned out after that before I ended up raging in the tiny cell and got stuck in there longer.

I must have fallen asleep at some point because I blinked my eyes open to the harsh, LED lighting coming through the open door.

"Learned your lesson, mutt?" Ronaldo's wheezing voice was like claws on a chalkboard.

I kept my mouth shut as I stood. My bones creaked and I cracked my neck. Sleeping sitting up when I couldn't shift was murder on my back. I stared down the councilor, waiting for him to tell me why he was releasing me from the hole rather than a guard. He didn't disappoint.

"You have one last chance to tell me where the princess is hiding, or I will use other means to find her." Ronaldo glared at me.

"I'm not telling you shit." I crossed my arms over my chest.

I couldn't tell him even if I wanted to. I have no idea where she is or if she's even alive. Don't even think that way. She has to be alive. I would feel it if she died.

"Fine. I warned you." Ronaldo waved a hand to the guard behind him. "Take him back to his cell."

The guard grabbed my arm roughly, squeezing it hard. He wasn't the same one who'd been helping me, but he wasn't one of the scared humans, either. He was Fae, and if there was any indication by his attitude, he bought right into Ronaldo's bullshit.

The guard shoved me when he could, pushing me into the wall and just all around manhandling me. It was to be expected that when we got back to my cell he shoved me against the bars.

"You're filth and we will eradicate you from the realms. We have already started the process." He shoved my face between the bars.

Fenrick stood with his hands balled into fists, but I shook my head as much as I was able. We didn't need anyone else ending up in the hole. We needed to get the fuck out of here.

The guard finally swiped the keycard over the scanner and the door slowly swung open. He shoved my back hard, and I stumbled into the cell moments before he slammed it closed behind me.

"You'll get yours, shifter scum," the guard called over his shoulder as he strolled away.

"You make friends everywhere you go, don't you?" Fenrick shook his head.

"It's part of my charm, I guess." I chuckled.

"Where did they take you?" Fenrick asked.

"The hole, just like he said. It's a tiny cell that's pitch black and boring as all hell, but I got some information from stupid human guards who didn't realize I could hear them through the steel door."

"What is it?" he asked warily.

"They are rounding all of us up and throwing away the keys," I huffed and dropped down on the cot.

"Genocide. I didn't even think the Council was that evil." Fenrick sat with his elbows on his knees.

"Look who runs the council. The guy who took pleasure in carving *shifter scum* on my body. Of course, they're that evil." I fell back on the cot, thankful that I could stretch out my legs finally.

"You're right—" Fenrick started to say more but I shushed him.

The sound of several pairs of footsteps making their way toward us reached my ears, and I stood abruptly. There had only been one time that I had to be escorted by more than one guard, and that was when they took me to Ronaldo's house of horrors.

This wasn't good at all. Was Ronaldo making good on his threat from earlier?

Two guards stepped to the cell and sneered at Fenrick through the bars. "You're coming with us, traitor."

"The hell he is." I stepped in front of Fenrick but knew it was futile.

"Don't get yourself in even more trouble, shifter scum. You want to go back to the hole?" the guard on the right said.

He swiped his badge over the scanner and stepped inside with one of those electrified batons the human guards had. He flicked it on, and the buzz of electricity met my ears.

"Where are you taking him?" I asked, throwing my hands up in surrender.

"The High Councilor wants to have a chat with him."

"Fuck, no. Take me instead." I took a step forward, but the man thrust the baton at me, and I had to hop back.

"Boss' orders we bring in the traitor. Now, you can get out of my way, or you can have electricity flood your system before I kick the shit out of you."

"It's okay, Grey. Stand down. I can take it." Fenrick patted my shoulder as he took a step around me.

I lunged at the guards but before I could get close Fenrick shoved me back on my ass. "Stop, Grey."

"He better come back from this." I roared. "I'm already planning each of your bloody deaths. If he doesn't come back, I'll torture you slowly when I get out of here!"

The guards didn't even spare me a glance as they took a resigned Fenrick from the cell and marched him down the hall.

Hopelessness ate my insides as the door closed behind them, locking me in with no way to help my friend.

Please let him come back.

CHAPTER 9

AURELIA

The TV in the corner of the room blared with the carnage that was Dallas. Humans were terrified of the knowledge that supernaturals existed and were acting out everywhere. It wasn't just locally, it was on a global scale.

One picture after another of people being beaten by gangs of humans who thought they were supernaturals flashed across the screen. The death toll was rising, and people were being accused without proof of being magical.

"It's a bloodbath," I whispered. "It's like the Salem witch trials all over again. Don't people ever learn?"

"No, Princess," Ash said softly. "They let their fear of the unknown rule them while some use it to their advantage to seek vengeance on those they feel wronged them."

"He's right," Zeke said never looking up from his screen as his fingers flew across the keyboard. "There are reports of people being beaten who had not a single drop of magical blood.

They were pointed out by jealous fools who wanted what they had."

"Or the hatred in their heart made them so angry that they would lash in any way they could to do the most damage." I sighed.

Why did people have to be so cruel? Why couldn't they stop this hatred of the unknown? They were supposed to be getting past all the bigotry and hatred, but every time something came along that they didn't understand, they lashed out.

The scene changed on the TV to a bunch of people throwing bottles at storefronts. My eyes widened as I realized they were outside a potion shop on the witch side of Dallas.

"What the hell are they doing?" I whispered, my eyes glued to the screen.

Asher ran a hand down his face. "It's been like this for a couple days now, Princess. They've been looting and rioting."

"But, why? What does that accomplish?" I asked.

"Absolutely nothing," Zeke groaned beside Ash. "They are tearing their own neighborhoods apart out of fear or just because they can."

"Humans make no sense," Ash grumbled.

"A witch just got mugged and beat nearly to death." Zeke never looked up from his laptop. "Instead of taking her to the hospital, they're holding her in one of those special facilities to be tested."

"That is so much bullshit." I leaned forward. "Did the people who hurt her at least get arrested?"

Zeke glanced at me over the screen and shook his head. "The police said she started it and let them all go."

"How can they do this? These are people we're talking

about, not monsters. Innocents are being treated like criminals out of fear and the real monsters can do stuff like this and get away with it." My hands tingled with my magic, and I clenched them into fists.

I couldn't let my anger get the better of me and trigger my magic. I was better than that and the guys didn't deserve the hassle of cleaning it up.

"Look at that sign." Kiernan said with a shake of his head. "*Animals belong in cages.* Complete bullshit when they are the ones acting like animals."

I peered at the sign and growled. Why did people have to be like that? This was all the Council's doing, and I made a promise to end their oppressive rule.

"This is what the Council wanted from the beginning. It will be easier to round up the supernaturals with the humans fear thick in the air," I said.

I knew how Ronaldo thought. He was the worst of all supernaturals for the way he was planning this.

"What do we do?" Kiernan asked. "How do we stop this?"

"We don't," Dan's voice sounded from the office door, startling me.

"Where have you been?" I jumped from my chair.

Dan had black circles under his eyes and his dark hair was sticking up at odd angles. He limped into the room and took a seat next to Ash.

"They're rounding up our people. Innocents with kids and families are disappearing into thin air." He ran a hand down his face.

"The government called for those actions," I said.

"I know, but two days ago I got a tip that an influential

shifter family was on the chopping block. Something about a political rival accusing them of being supernatural. They were going to be raided, and this is the only safe place for us in the realm now."

"Nowhere else is safe?" I asked in horror.

I glanced back at the TV screen, watching the people riot and loot once again. They didn't care that they were hurting others. They were hurting other humans to get back at supernaturals and for what? What was the purpose of any of the senseless violence?

"Shifter side is completely deserted. They're all gone, and I don't know if it's because someone tipped them off, or if everyone left when the raids started happening." Dan tilted his head back and huffed out a breath of frustration.

"What about the witches? This has to be fucking terrible for them," I said, running a hand through my hair.

"The witches have been hiding. Their side of town looks abandoned, but only because it's like a no man's land now. Someone informed them where to find the communities of supernaturals and that's where they went first."

"Shit. Malcolm. He's lived here long enough to know where the communities are and who the big players are. He would have tipped them off." I shook my head.

"Malcolm." Kiernan turned sharply to me. "Your betrothed?"

I held up my hand to ward off that particular conversation. "Don't start with that. I will never marry that creep."

Kiernan nodded and turned back to the TV, thankfully ending that subject. I didn't want to ever speak of it again. I had my mate.

"Yes, I believe Malcolm tipped them off on quite a bit, but we are extracting as many as we can when we get a tip telling us who might be next," Dan said. "It just takes a lot of manpower."

"Is that why you left those idiots in charge?" I asked with a raised brow.

Dan flinched. "Sorry about that, Aurelia. They know better now than to do anything like that to you again. I told them I would let the trolls have them for punching bags if I ever heard such disrespect again."

"Grey would have lost his mind and done something similar to what happened to Layla." I shuddered.

"About Grey," Dan said slowly.

"Do you know where he is?" I gasped, jumping from my chair.

"I do. I have a man inside the maximum-security prison, and he has eyes on Grey and your father."

I flopped back in my chair, slumping in my seat. They were in prison here in the human realm and no doubt it was a similar set-up as the jail they broke the shifter out of. "How are we going to get them out?"

"I don't know yet, but at least we know they're alive, Princess." Dan patted my hand.

There was a time I would have recoiled and probably slapped him for having the nerve to touch me after what he'd done, but that had passed with all the help he'd given me since.

"He thinks I'm dead," I whispered.

Tears burned behind my eyes. I hated it. I didn't want to show weakness, but the thought that my mate might have been hurting because he thought I was dead gutted me.

Asher glanced at me from his spot at the table going through reports. "I'm sure he can tell you're still alive from the bond you share."

"How can you know that?" I asked, but Ash just shook his head.

Was there a story there? Did the big man have a mate in the past? What happened to her? I wanted to ask the questions out loud, but Ash's eyes hardened, and he turned back to his papers.

"It's just a shifter thing," Zeke said instead. "Shifters have fated mates but some of us do not."

My shoulders curled in on me as I peered down at my lap. This was not the conversation we needed to be having. We needed to be focused on getting Grey out of that prison.

"Anyway, we need a plan or something to get Grey out of there." I crossed my arms over my chest. "How hard can it be to break into a human prison?"

"That's the problem, Aurelia. The warden fired half his men so that Ronaldo's own guards are there along with the humans. It's the only reason I have eyes in there." Dan looked away from my hopeful expression as it fell.

"How does Ronaldo have so much influence that he can just get away with all of this?" I threw my hands up in the air and stood.

Zeke glanced up from his laptop. "Think about it. The human government knows that shifters are stronger than humans, and that witches have powers unthinkable to them."

He sat back and waited for his words to sink in. "They can't lock us up because we're more powerful, so they need traitors like Ronaldo to keep the peace in those facilities."

"Bingo. It wasn't about Ronaldo's influence, it was about the human government's need to have security for the humans and this is what they came up with." Zeke rubbed his eyes with his thumb and forefinger.

"You're the smart one, aren't you?" I grinned.

Ash scoffed. "If he's the smart one, then I'm the sexy one."

"Right," Zeke coughed a laugh.

I rolled my eyes, but Ash's comment hit its mark, and I chuckled. I still didn't understand how anyone could be scared of the giant teddy bears that were Asher and Zeke.

"I bet the human guards aren't happy about losing their jobs and it's adding fuel to the fire." I pointed to the TV, where a sign talked about supernaturals taking over the world and making humans slaves.

"That is definitely Ronaldo's plan, but I don't get how he's going to pull it off." Zeke glanced at the screen before turning back to whatever research he was conducting.

"He doesn't just want the humans as slaves, though. He wants everyone to be slaves to the Council and too many Fae are jumping on his bandwagon. If we don't do something, we're going to lose this war and possibly everything we love." I sighed.

"We need to come up with a plan to stop him. No matter what, he can't be allowed to enslave everyone in the realms." Dan leaned forward on his elbows.

"You didn't see what I saw in Faery when he captured Grey and the others. He took over my father's entire castle. If the knights didn't swear an oath, they said they were imprisoned but when I went to the dungeons, no one was there. They were empty." I covered my face with my hands.

Ash slammed his hands down on the table, startling me. "We're looking at this the wrong way. We need to tackle this one problem at a time."

I gasped when I glanced at the TV, seeing what had Ash riled. They had a little girl no more than eight years old crying for her mother as they shoved her in the back of a cop car for no crime other than being born a shifter.

"That's barbaric. She's just a child." I jumped from my chair, clenching my fists angrily at my sides.

"Until we can figure out how to stop this, we need to figure out how we can protect the innocent. They don't deserve to be locked in cells and tested. They don't understand what's happening her." Ash turned angry eyes on Zeke.

"I'm on it. I can hack in and make sure we get access to who they are going for next." Zeke tapped away at his computer.

I hoped he could do what he said, and we could get the supernaturals to safety because my heart broke for that little girl that reminded me so much of myself.

CHAPTER 10

GREY

Where the fuck is Fenrick? It's been too long. Why isn't he back yet?

I had nothing to do but pace the empty cell and wait for any news on what had happened to my friend. If Ronaldo killed him, he would suffer my wrath.

My shoulders slumped in defeat. I couldn't do anything to the councilor while locked in cell with those damn cuffs on my wrists.

I couldn't plan any kind of escape until I knew Fenrick was safe. He would be getting out of this with us. There was no other option.

I tugged at the ends of my unwashed hair as I continued to pace. Who else had Ronaldo been torturing? Were the king and Magna okay?

What lengths would Ronaldo go to in order to get his hands on my mate and my facility? They may have been the only ones who could help us stop Ronaldo and his reign of terror.

Slow, methodical footsteps sounded coming down the cell block, and I tensed. There was only one man this time, so it couldn't have been them bringing Fenrick back from his torture session with Ronaldo.

The same guard from before stopped just outside my cell and stared at me with a raised brow.

"Time to go to the mess hall," he said.

My stomach rumbled as if on cue, and I grimaced. How long had it been since I'd eaten anything? I couldn't even remember. I didn't get a chance the last time we were there. Not that I would call what they'd served in the mess hall food.

He swiped his badge and the buzzing of the door being opened screeched through the cell. Reluctantly, I followed, and he grabbed my arm roughly, pulling me into his side.

"I don't have to tell you again what will happen if you start more fights, right?" His gaze flicked up to the security camera at the end of the hall and back to me with a warning scowl.

"I told you I didn't pick that fight. I have no intention of going back to the hole." I played along, yanking at my arm in his grip.

"I also said last time that it didn't matter who started it. You will be sent back to the hole and if your rumbling stomach is any indication on how starving you are, you won't last the week sentence." He yanked on my arm again.

"Understood."

He wasn't wrong. There was no way I would survive another day without food. I wasn't stupid. I had no intention of dying in that place.

"Are you trying to fight me now?" He sneered.

He was really good at pretending he hated my guts and everything I stood for.

"No. I thought you were taking me to the mess hall, traitor." I threw the last word in for effect.

I had called every other Fae guard some version of that, so it would be suspicious if I didn't call him the same.

He yanked me back so we were nose-to-nose, my back was to the camera, and he slipped something into my pocket. I stiffened but kept my glare firmly in place for the cameras.

"I would watch who you call a traitor in this place, *Shifter King.*" He spat out the words.

"Everyone in this place will get what they deserve before the end of this. *Everyone,*" I said as both a promise and a threat.

He was helping as much as he was able to so he wouldn't face my wrath, but every other Fae and human in this place keeping us chained because we were different would.

He pushed my back, shoving me down the hall. His mission was complete, but I didn't dare take note of what was in my pocket until I was back in my cell. It could get us both in serious trouble.

None of the other inmates had an escort through the prison, and I narrowed my eyes on the guard.

He shrugged. "You're a flight risk and a troublemaker. We have been told to have eyes on you constantly when you're outside your cell."

That made sense. Ronaldo knew me better than I thought, because I would escape at the first opportunity. What he hadn't realized was that I had a man on the inside, and as long as it was safe to do so, the guard was going to help us escape.

"Fair enough." I strolled through the doors to the mess hall and got in line for whatever it was they passed off as food in this place.

I scanned the room. There were groups of inmates clustered around tables, but I quickly realized there was a divide. Groups without cuffs on their wrists were the human criminals who belonged there and there weren't many of them.

Had they shipped the humans off to other prisons to make this a supernatural prison? If so, then why did they keep human guards around? They probably didn't have enough Fae to do the job.

The line was quick, and I easily found Magna and the Shadow King at a table off to the side by themselves.

"What the hell happened to you?" I asked.

Magna had a black bruise around her eye and her shoulders were hunched. The Shadow King wasn't much better. Beneath the collar of his shirt were thin red lines like he'd been sliced open.

"That bastard Ronaldo took great pleasure in slicing me up," the king said, adjusting his collar.

I dropped my tray to the table with a loud clatter and growled low in my throat. That bastard was going to pay for what he was doing to us.

"Where's Fenrick?" the king asked, searching the mess hall.

"Probably the same place you both were. It was maybe an hour after they released me from the hole that he was taken to Ronaldo, and I haven't seen him since." I ran a hand down my face and plopped down on the bench seat across from them.

"He's making his way through all of us then." The king sighed.

"What questions did he ask?"

"He asked me where the passageways in the castle led and where is Aurelia. One of his guards said he spotted her in the library, but they can't find her. He also asked about the facility's location." The king picked his fork up and grimaced at his plate.

My heart leapt with the news that someone had seen her. Could she really be alive? Was she running from the Council?

"They think they saw her?" I asked, not daring to hope but also my heart was lighter.

My wolf perked up his ears and whimpered, wanting his mate back with him. He wasn't the only one, but we had to get out of this place to find her.

"Yes, but that's not entirely good either. If they saw her, that means she's stuck in Faery. She can't sift yet." The king took a bite of the gruel.

"Shit. I hadn't thought of that. They probably have guards all over the castle." I turned to Magna. "What did he ask you?"

"It was strange, like he knew who I was and what I could do. He asked me a lot of questions about the future. He also asked me about Aurelia." Her eyes were glassy for a moment.

"How could he know about your secret? That is something we've carefully guarded over the years." I grabbed the stale roll off my plate and tore it in half.

"He knows way too much for my comfort," Magna agreed.

"I think he's getting frustrated that no one will tell him what he wants to know." I grinned.

"That's dangerous, though." The king eyed me over his fork. "Frustration and anger lead to recklessness, and he could go too far with Fenrick."

I tightened my fist around the roll and flattened it. "His

death will be mine either way, but if Fenrick doesn't come back to the cell, I will torture him slowly before I end his miserable existence."

Magna blinked at me then glanced over at the huge shifter from the other day. "Befriend the bear."

"What?" I asked warily. "You want me to befriend the shifter who got me Tased and thrown in the hole?"

"It's important, Grey. You need to befriend the bear shifter."

"Magna, you do realize how crazy that sounds, right? If I go over there right now, he's going to get aggressive again, and I'm going to get a week in the hole. None of us can afford that." I shook my head.

The Shadow King glanced over his shoulder and frowned at the big shifter who was glaring at me with hate filled eyes.

"Those are not the eyes of someone who wants to be friends." The king shook his head and turned back to us.

"You need to befriend the bear," Magna warned again.

"Can I eat first?" I asked. "Last time I didn't even get a chance to eat before I was thrown in the hole."

They never gave me shit to eat in the hole and despite how disgusted I was with the food in the mess hall, I couldn't go much longer without fuel.

My stomach rumbled angrily, and the king grinned.

"I'm surprised you aren't rabid. With your shifter metabolism, you need to eat a lot more than the rest of us." The king popped a piece of roll into his mouth.

"Well with these cuffs on, I can't shift. I think that's the only thing that's kept me from losing my shit completely."

The king nodded to me. I didn't need my shifter metabolism

if I couldn't shift and for the first time, I was grateful to not have my magic. If I had it, I never would have survived the hunger.

I ate in silence until everything was cleared from my tray. It wasn't enough but it would get me through. Magna smiled and handed me her roll. I nodded my thanks and bit into it with a savage hunger.

"We need to figure out a way out of here," I whispered. "They are calling me a flight risk, so I have a guard watching me at all times."

"I noticed that. There are several tense now, watching your every move," the king said.

"I don't know how, but we need to escape." I steepled my fingers in front of my lips.

"Befriend the bear," Magna said again.

"You think that will help?" I asked.

How could befriending a psychotic shifter who wanted to fight me help us get out of the hellhole we were in? It didn't make sense, but that was all the information I was getting from Magna. She always was cryptic.

"Yes, it's the catalyst. Befriend the bear." Magna nodded to the shifter who was still glaring daggers at me.

"Fine, I get it. You won't stop until I do what I'm told." I pushed myself up off the bench and walked toward the shifter.

The room went eerily silent as the entire mess hall stared, holding their breath to see what I was doing. I sauntered up to the shifter's table and grinned at him. The bear frowned and growled like he was more bear than man.

"What do you want?" he asked.

He clenched his hand into a fist as he stood from the bench

but in a second, I was surrounded. Ten shifters circled around me, boxing me in.

The guards stepped away from the walls, all of them tense. They were waiting for the inevitable.

I was about to get mauled by a pack of angry shifters and locked in the hole again. Just fucking great.

CHAPTER 11

AURELIA

"Aurelia!" my mother yelled as she burst into the office. She scanned the room and her face fell when she didn't see who she was looking for.

"I'm sorry," I said. "They're alive but in a human prison."

My mother erupted into tears and hugged me to her. It was still awkward, but I was getting better now that I had my memories back.

"I'm just glad you're safe," she sniffled.

"We're going to get them back, Mother. We have to." I patted her back.

I glanced around at all the men in the room. They were the best shot we had at planning a prison break in a maximum-security facility. They would have my back every step of the way, and I was grateful for that.

"I know you will. You are so strong and determined. How can I help?" she asked, taking a step back and swiping at her eyes.

"I need you to stay here and help with the people we rescue. There are families with children Ben brought in, and they need to know where they're not allowed for safety reasons. This isn't a facility meant for children, and we will need to block off any rooms that house weapons."

It was the only thing I could think of because I didn't think my mother was equipped for a prison break and we only had one shot at this. We needed the best of our team to pull it off.

"I can handle that." She nodded firmly.

Good. I was afraid she was going to argue about going on the rescue mission with us, and I would have to get one of the guys to back me up or lock her away somewhere.

If it was me and they were telling me I couldn't go, they would have to lock me up to keep me away.

I turned back to the group with a determined frown. "Okay, where were we?"

Zeke turned turquoise eyes on me. "I think I can get into the mainframe but the supernaturals there aren't listed. I'm looking at the government's lists too, but Grey and Fenrick aren't on that list either. It's like they never existed."

"How can Ronaldo get away with this? He can just lock them in a prison without a trace. It shouldn't be allowed." I flopped into the chair.

How the hell were we supposed to get them out if we didn't know where to look?

Ash scrubbed a hand down his face. "He has friends in some very high places if he can pull that off."

"There are laws against this sort of thing. He could be doing anything he wants to them there because according to the rest of the world, they aren't even there." I slammed my fist on the desk.

My shadow magic rose up and swirled angrily around my arms. It was coming easier to me lately. It also got out of control, like now when I didn't call it but emotions were high.

Zeke glared at his laptop screen. "They don't see us as human, so their laws don't apply to us."

"Oh?" I asked with a grin. "If their laws don't apply to us, they can't detain us."

"I would say that as well," Asher said, though I could hear the *but* coming. "But if the Council has declared themselves our governing body, we would have to abide by the Council's rule and they can detain us."

"Why'd you have to burst my bubble so fast?" I pouted.

I thought I had found a loophole to their idiotic reasoning but of course, the Council had named themselves our government as soon as they overtook my father's castle and taken out Nicholas.

"Sorry, Princess," Ash chuckled. "It's what makes the most sense."

"I know it makes sense, but I was getting all sorts of ideas. There have to be some people reacting differently to this, right? Are any civil rights attorneys standing up for us?" I asked, turning to Zeke.

"There has been some people speaking out in support, but they are labeled sympathizers, and some have supernatural spouses or children, and it's making life difficult for them." Zeke turned his screen to me.

The article was a political hit piece talking about shifter

sympathizers being arrested for speaking out against the government and hiding their loved ones.

"This is fucking insanity," I whispered.

"It is, but this is our life unless we do something about it." Asher clenched his fist, his gaze hard on mine.

"We are willing to stop this, no matter what it takes. The Council will be ended. I will end them myself, if I have to," I growled.

Dan rushed in the room, his eyes wild. "Turn on the TV. They're about to make an announcement."

"What kind of announcement?" I jumped from my chair and raced to the TV turning it on forgetting that there was a remote to the thing.

"They are making a presidential announcement about the existence of supernaturals and what the government plans to do about the *problem*." Dan planted his hand on his hips.

"Problem?" I shrieked. "Our people have been living among them for centuries peacefully, and now we're a problem?"

"It's fear, Aurelia. That's all it is." Dan patted my shoulder.

"I don't care about their fear." I narrowed my eyes at the screen.

The podium stood empty waiting for the President to address the nation. There was a box live streaming in the corner, showing more of the lawlessness in the major cities around the country. It was all being blamed on us, like we just showed up out of nowhere and started trouble.

"The looting and rioting isn't us. It's the human reaction to us. How is that our fault?" I asked, deflating.

"It's not, but the government is in a tight spot with so many people demanding regulations on supernaturals around the globe." Zeke rubbed his neck.

Dan stepped forward, shushing us and pointing to the screen. A group of people filed into view behind the President of the United States.

"Good morning to all Americans. Some troubling news has come to light in the recent weeks. We are doing everything to protect the American people. Not to be confused with the beings we have recently discovered that live among us." The President paused and held up his hand to quiet the reporters in the crowd.

"I will take questions after I'm done with my statement. This very troubling news has a silver lining. We can learn from these creatures to better the human race."

"You mean test on us, you piece of shit!" I yelled.

"All supernaturals must submit to be registered with the Department of Homeland Security and sent to our intake facilities where they will be evaluated to find out if they are safe to live among humans in this country. If they are deemed unsafe, they will be remanded to maximum-security prisons throughout the country."

"I bet those *intake facilities* are labs, and no one ever leaves once they are there." I growled.

"The Department of Justice will be conducting random raids on any individuals suspected of being supernatural. It will be better for everyone if you all turn yourselves in, rather than making us waste valuable time and resources to track you all down. The consequences will be severe and assets you own may be seized if you do not comply with the new laws."

He opened the floor to questions, and I turned terrified eyes on the guys. "This is so much worse than I could have imagined."

"It's like Nazi Germany. They are moving backward." Ash stood about to turn the TV off, but I stopped him.

"I want to see if anyone asks the right questions."

The President pointed to a woman in the front, and she stood. "Isn't this a bit extreme?" she asked. "They have been living among us long enough to have homes and families and businesses."

They turned the camera back on the President. "No, this isn't extreme. Have you seen the protests and fighting that your station plays on repeat? These creatures are dangerous and until we can explain more about them, they should be registered as supernatural."

"But, Mr. President, This looks a lot like Germany before World War II. Shouldn't we be more understanding than just locking them up."

"Are you sympathizing with these creatures?" he asked the journalist, and she gasped.

"No, I just wonder how far down this slippery slope you're willing to go. Do human Americans that don't fit into your norms have to worry about this happening to them? How will these suspected supernaturals be identified? Can just anyone with a grudge report someone? There are too many variables to consider."

"I'm glad you asked that question. We will have reporting centers open at all local police stations. There will be a verified staff member there who can spot the lie, and should someone falsely accuse another of being one of these creatures they will be penalized under the new laws."

"They are going to have Fae at the police stations to tell when people are lying? Bullshit." I flopped back in my chair over this façade of a press conference.

The President called on a man in the front next. "Mr. President, do you have any words for the human individuals who are rioting and looting in the streets over this tricky situation?"

"I want my fellow Americans to know that the conduct that we have seen in our cities over the last few days is unacceptable. I am prepared to send out the National Guard to stop these people from behaving in such a way. All violators will be punished harshly under the law. Stop rioting and looting. We are taking care of the problem."

"Wait!" I yelled and turned, fumbling for the remote.

I rewound to the correct place. The flash of magic filled the screen and I paused. "What the fuck is he doing with the President of the United States?"

I pointed to the corner where Malcolm stood behind the President, his eyes sparking with his magic.

Everyone in the room threw out a litany of curses that would make a sailor blush. Is that what Ronaldo had meant in the dungeon of the castle about the human government?

"Is mind control an actual thing?" I turned to my mother.

She nodded. "It's not done, though. Fae children are taught at a young age how to shield themselves from mind control so there was never really a point in trying."

"Humans don't know, nor do they have the power to shield their minds. Fuck." I groaned.

I tilted my head back and squeezed my eyes shut. This was fucking bad. I couldn't even hate on the President or call him prejudiced because this wasn't him. He was being controlled by a sadist who wanted to take over the world.

The only sound in the room was Zeke's rhythmic tapping on the keyboard in front of him. "This doesn't really change anything."

"Doesn't it?" I asked, turning my gaze on him.

"Not really. We still need to get Grey and the others out and stop the Council's crazy." Zeke shrugged.

Dan leaned down on the table, locking eyes with me. "I think we are looking at this all wrong."

"What do you mean?" I asked.

"Knowing this might not be the President's agenda but the agenda of the Council, all we would have to do to stop the registration of supernaturals is to cut off the Council's influence." Dan's eyes were wide.

"I don't know. What if we cut off their influence and to save face, the President continues or decides on a worse plan?" I chewed my lip nervously. "What if instead of testing on us, they decide genocide is the better option?"

It was a very real concern, considering the human population was much bigger than ours. How could we expect to fight against armies of billions and win?

CHAPTER 12

GREY

I crouched into a fighting stance and spun around, eyeing the shifters around me. I didn't recognize any of them and I couldn't really just from the back of their heads.

The bear shifter growled and took a menacing step forward, and the others closed ranks around me, boxing me in.

What the hell is going on here? Are they protecting me from the bear? I don't need protection.

"Look, I don't want to cause any trouble. I thought we could be allies," I said, but the snarling of the wolves around me drowned out my voice.

"You want to be allies?" The big shifter laughed. "Why would I want to be allies with the disgraced Shifter King's brat?"

"Because he wasn't disgraced. He was set up by the same people who locked us in here." I eyed him.

He wasn't going to buy it, and that was fine. I could at least tell Magna that I tried. The guards inched closer to us with their batons, and I scanned the room warily. I didn't want them to hear what I had to say to the supernaturals in the room.

"What's going on here?" the guard from before shouted.

My shoulders stiffened as I turned to face him. I was not picking a damn fight this time. I had no idea why the shifters surrounded me.

"Nothing. I was trying to make amends." I put my hands up in surrender, not wanting to get another shock like last time.

Out of the corner of my eye the Shadow King stood ready to jump in and help if needed, but I shook my head just as Magna tugged on his arm to make him sit down.

What was she up to? She obviously saw this and knew it needed to be done, but I was so confused. The entire mess hall was silent again.

The guard nodded to the snarling shifters around me that had yet to take their gazes off the bear shifter.

"Stand down. You don't want to go to the hole. Trust me!" I barked at the shifters.

The ten shifters all whimpered, and their shoulders slumped. They stepped back from the bear with their necks bared to me. They really were trying to protect me when I walked up to the bear.

"See?" I waved a hand at the gathered group. "No problems here."

The bear sat back in his seat and crossed his arms over his chest. The guard raised an eyebrow at the bear, and he shook his head.

"We were just having a chat."

The guard took a step back and waved a hand for the other guards to step back against the wall.

The shifters around me shuffled their feet, their heads still down and necks bared.

"What the hell were you all doing causing a scene like that?" I asked.

The biggest one who stood directly in front of me turned, and I recognized him as someone from the Syndicate.

"Sorry, boss. After I saw you get Tased the other day, I couldn't let it happen again. I know you of all people will have a plan to get us out of here." The shifter's eyes shone with his wolf.

"I'm working on it," I mumbled.

I hated having all their hopes resting on my shoulders, but I would figure something out. We would not be there long. I would make sure of it.

"You have a plan?" The bear shifter sat forward with his elbows on the table in front of him.

He didn't seem like much of a team player. When I'd seen him in the mess hall he was sitting on his own glaring at anyone who dared come close.

"I said I'm working on it. You will all know when it's time to go." I spun on my heel and stomped back to Magna and the Shadow King.

I glared at Magna but there was no heat in it. I couldn't stay mad at the woman. She'd been too helpful over the years.

"Was that so hard?" She grinned.

"Considering I thought I was about to get Tased again if I couldn't defuse the situation? Yes," I said.

"Grey, we need all the help we can get for when the time comes," she whispered.

Apparently the shifters who protected me had followed me because they filled in the seats at the table around me.

"You are the most powerful shifter in this place, Shifter King. That's why Brutus attacked you. His bear was threatened." The shifter I'd recognized from the Syndicate ducked his head.

The one next to me stared at me with hopeful eyes. "We request protection. Some of the warlocks have been raging on us, saying it's our fault this happened and there are many more of them here. They don't fight fair, and attack in groups while the guards aren't looking."

"If you're requesting protection, why try to protect me?" I asked. "That doesn't even make any sense."

I ran a hand through my hair and stared at Magna and the Shadow King, who were doing their best not to burst into laughter at my discomfort as several other shifters came up behind me offering their rolls and whatever else they had, requesting protection.

Shit. This was stupid. Why couldn't they just stick to packs instead of pinning all their hopes on me?

The shifter from the Syndicate huffed. "You're our best chance of escaping and waging war on the Fae. I told them all this because you have the Syndicate, and your army there is loyal to you. These shifters will be loyal as well. We just have to figure out a way out of here first."

"I'm working on it," I said for what felt like the thousandth time.

If only I could work on it a little faster.

My tray was full again and instead of arguing, I accepted

their loyalty and promised them whatever protection I could give.

Shifters weren't to blame for outing supernaturals to the humans. The Fae Council was, and I would be letting the warlocks in the prison know that immediately.

We weren't enemies, but we did have a common enemy, and I would use that knowledge to get the warlocks off the shifters' backs.

"Where are these warlocks?" I asked the shifter next to me.

He nodded to a table in the opposite corner of the mess hall. Shit. That wasn't good. If the guards saw me walking over there after the scene I just made, I could end up in the hole again, but the supernaturals in this place needed to stick together not bully each other.

I stood from my seat and several guards around the walls tensed as I walked around the room to the warlock table. The man in the middle of the table smirked at me as I leaned over.

"You've been harassing my shifters. Why?" I asked with a growl.

"A shifter is the reason we're in this place in the first place," the warlock said.

"It could have easily been a witch or warlock that was caught. The Council selected the wolf specifically for the most dramatic effect. Think about it. Why are the Fae in this building holding us prisoner?" I asked.

The warlock arched a brow and scratched his chin. Maybe this was the first time he'd listened to sense about this and not his own raging at being sent to prison for what he was.

"My people broke the shifter out of jail, and he told me that he smelled something chemical before he lost control. I know that the Fae are working with the humans to make us all their slaves. I've spoken to the *High Councilor* myself. The man is like any superhero villain's endless monologue about his plans for world domination."

The warlock leaned forward, studying me like he thought I was lying, but something in my expression must have told him the truth.

"We've been lied to and persecuted before. Why should we trust a shifter?" He asked.

"Because I have the means to get us out of here and take the Council down. Ever heard of the Syndicate?" I asked, and shocked gasps echoed around the table.

"You're not the boss of the Syndicate." The warlock sneered.

"You believe I'm the Shifter King, but I couldn't possibly be the owner of the Syndicate?" I smirked.

"I wouldn't believe that either, if all the shifters hadn't been whispering about it since you arrived," the warlock said.

"Honestly, I don't care what you believe, but we need to stick together in here, not torture each other. Ronaldo does enough of that as it is." I shook my head.

The warlocks glanced warily between each other as I said the High Councilor's name without his title.

"The High Councilor is torturing people?" one of the warlocks whispered.

"Only every day. A friend was taken to him yesterday and he's yet to come back." I glanced between the warlocks, letting them see how serious this was.

I wasn't lying that we all needed to stick together and that I was going to get us out of here.

"Okay," the warlock in the middle said. "You said you were going to get us out of here."

"I can't tell you how or when, just stop harassing my shifters and be ready." I leaned forward on my elbows.

"We'll leave the shifters alone." The warlock nodded.

"Good." I pushed up from the bench seat and moved back to the table with Magna, the fae king and the shifters.

I sat down in my seat and nodded to the everyone. "They won't harass you anymore or they're getting left behind when we get out of here."

"You're really planning to break us all out?" one whispered.

"Yes, we have to stop the Council. They can't be allowed to continue what they're doing." I clenched my hand on the table.

"Shifter King!" someone called, and I turned to find the guard standing behind me. "Time to go back to your cell."

No one else moved but I stood from the bench, pocketing a couple rolls as I did and let the guard manhandle me out of the mess hall while everyone else watched.

"That was reckless," the guard whispered.

"It wasn't. I have a seer on my side who told me to do it." I shook my head.

"She shouldn't be able to see through the cuffs." He squeezed my arm.

We stomped between the cells on our way back to mine.

"Well, she's half Fae, half witch, so I don't think even Ronaldo knows how to handle her." I yanked my arm away from him.

"Interesting. You've surrounded yourself with people who are extremely useful." The guard nodded.

"It's how I made my fortune in this realm, and it's how I'm going to get us all out of this mess."

I didn't tell him my mate was really the one who was going to get us out of this. We all knew she was the one that was destined to take down the Council.

When we got back to my cell, he swiped his badge and the cell buzzed as the door swung open. My shoulders slumped as I trudged into the empty space.

"Try to keep a low profile," the guard said as he closed me in.

"How do you expect me to do that when I have shifters requesting protection?" I asked and scanned the cell hoping I'd been wrong, and Fenrick was really there.

No Fenrick. Where the hell is he? What is that sadist doing to him and how the hell are we supposed to get out of here when he's disappeared?

CHAPTER 13

AURELIA

"We need to call a meeting," I said to Dan and the guys.

"Why?" Dan asked.

"We need to lock down the building. Only authorized personnel should be able to leave and only those that can spot a tail. We can't lead them back to us."

"Smart." Ash nodded. "They are targeting supernaturals, and anyone not trained to watch for someone following them could lead the government right to us."

The sound of Zeke tapping on keys filled the silence that stretched between us. "We've been getting to most of the innocents before the government but what happens when the building reaches capacity?"

"I don't know." I admitted. "We might have to think about having the witches and warlocks build more temporary housing. That will be harder to control though." I leaned back in the chair.

Every day I missed Grey more, and prayed to whatever gods that were listening that he was okay. I needed to get him out, but I had to secure the building and the people we were helping first, or he would have nothing to come back to.

"Okay," Dan said. "I'll call a mandatory meeting, but we have teams out in the field so not everyone will be there."

"That's fine. This doesn't apply to the extraction teams." I nodded.

Dan rushed from the room to call the meeting with all the residents quickly filling the space. It was getting seriously crowded, but we were beating the Council more often than not when it came to hiding people the government was raiding.

"I think I got something!" Zeke shouted.

"What is it?" I asked.

I jumped from my seat and rounded the table to peer over his shoulder.

"Schematics. They'd been deleted from the prison's server recently, but I was able to recover them."

"Why would they delete something like that? Don't they have to keep them by law?" I asked.

"I guess since they're making it a supernatural prison the laws don't apply." Zeke rubbed his eyes.

"Bastards," I grumbled. "They don't want any supernaturals to get any information to break in. They know it won't keep us all out of there. How are they even keeping them in there?"

"I found something that might explain it," Zeke mumbled. "There is a patent for a new type of cuff in the US Patent Office. It blocks magic."

Ash's head snapped up to his brother. "They patented magic-blocking handcuffs? When was it filed?"

"Six months ago."

"Shit. They've been planning this a long time." Ash clenched his hands into fists on the table.

I deflated and sat heavily back in my chair. "How are we going to do this when they've been planning for so long?"

"Because we have the one thing they couldn't control." Ash grinned at me.

"And what's that?" I asked, hoping he didn't say what I thought he was going to say.

"You, Aurelia. You're the one thing that they couldn't control no matter how hard they tried. They literally had you kidnapped as a child so you wouldn't be able to stop their plans. So, while yes, they have been planning this longer than any of us would have guessed, you are the one thing that can stop them."

"I was afraid you were going to say that. No pressure," I sighed.

Dan ran into the room panting. "Everyone is gathered for the meeting."

"That was fast." I nodded to Zeke and Ash.

We all filed into the elevator down the hall. "Is there a way to change the wards to keep everyone in?"

"The only one who can make changes to the wards is Grey," Dan said, hanging his head.

"Well, at least we can use that. They have to be escorted into the wards by someone who's authorized to be here in order to get in, so if they leave without permission, they won't be able to return." I leaned back against the wall of the elevator.

The elevator dinged when we got to the first floor. I rolled my shoulders back and followed Dan into the last room I had ever wanted to enter again, but it was where they held meetings as well as fights.

I blew out a nervous breath and followed Dan to the center of the room. The bleachers were full of stunned supernaturals. There were even people standing along the walls, glancing around nervously, clutching children to their chests.

"Thank you all for coming on short notice!" Dan yelled over the whispering crowd. "We have an announcement to make."

Dan nodded to me. I exhaled deeply and took a step forward. "Many of you know the dire situation in which we find ourselves. Many of you were extracted from your homes before the government could arrest you and take you to their testing facilities or lock you in a prison cell."

People nodded but started fidgeting like they were uncomfortable. It was an uncomfortable topic.

"From now until we stop the Council and return home to Faery, the facility is on lockdown. I understand this may be concerning to some. We will still be sending extraction teams to retrieve supernaturals before the government can get to them, but only those teams are allowed to leave."

The whispers turned to grumbling and a few called out that it was bullshit. Dan and the guys stepped up on either side of me with their arms crossed over their chests.

"Anyone who doesn't like it is free to leave and never return. You can take your chances with the testing facilities and the human government!" Dan barked.

The crowd silenced. Zeke pointed at a man in slacks and a button-down shirt. "Are you trained to watch for a tail?"

The man frowned and shook his head. "No."

"If you left and came back, you could lead the Council or

the human government to everyone here, yourself included. This is for your safety as well as everyone here."

Dan cut in. "This has never been a civilian facility. We have highly trained operatives that we send out into the world on various jobs. They are experts at making sure they aren't being followed. No one leaves except for authorized personnel. If you leave without permission, you will not be able to return."

Ash gripped my shoulder. "And if you think this is a joke and leave anyway and lead someone to our wards, retribution will be swift and brutal. Do not put the lives of innocents on the line because you think you're better than the rest of us. I will not be lenient if we are found."

I glanced at Ash with a frown. That was a little overboard, but the crowd didn't argue, and I was thankful for that as we stomped from the room and back to the elevator.

"Do you think they'll listen?" I asked when the doors closed behind us.

"Most of them will, but I noticed a few cocky assholes in the crowd who will probably try to leave to test us. They'll be handled." Ash crossed his arms over his chest and glared at the wall.

"They will just be one less person to worry about, Aurelia," Dan said.

"You can't save everyone," I agreed. "I'm just worried they'll lead the government right to us."

We wandered into the office, and the TV was blaring with the news we almost constantly had on now. It was pretty morbid. I shouldn't have watched it so much, but I needed to know what was happening.

"Are supernaturals finding a place to hide?" the newscaster

asked. "Three sting operations to capture these creatures came up completely empty yesterday here in Dallas."

I grinned and glanced between the guys. Their smiles were smug. "They're noticing that it's not just a fluke."

"The Department of Justice put out a statement early this morning warning that anyone caught aiding supernaturals will be brought up on charges of aiding and abetting a felon and placed in prison."

"They would have to catch us first." Ash chuckled.

I sat in the chair behind the desk and shook my head. "They would put us in prison or a facility either way. Charge me with the crime of saving innocents."

"Maybe we should think about that as an opportunity to break into the prison. Are we looking at this the wrong way?" Zeke mumbled.

"What do you mean?" I asked.

Was he suggesting we get arrested and hope that they send us to the correct place?

"I'm looking at these schematics and I can't find a way in except through the front door." Zeke scrubbed a hand over his face.

"We don't even know that they would take us to the correct facility if we got arrested." Ash said what I was thinking.

"It's too risky," I agreed.

"This whole mission is too risky, but we're still doing it." Zeke argued.

"How do we do that and ensure we're going to the right place though? We can't. We have no idea how they choose who goes where and we only have one shot at this." I tilted my head back and squeezed my eyes shut.

"We can't. I say if there's only one way in we blow the door open and go in guns blazing." Ash flopped in his seat.

"You always were the *blow shit up and ask questions later* kind," Zeke huffed.

"Do you have a better idea?" Ash threw a wadded-up piece of paper at him. "And not the one where we all get arrested and possibly split up to be tested on and caged."

Zeke hung his head. "No, but if we just go and blow shit up, we're going to need a large team to evacuate at multiple entry points, and there's only one way in and out."

Dan sat forward. "We have specialized teams for things just like this. The team that got the shifter out of jail was quick and efficient."

"What about your guy on the inside? Will he be able to help?" I asked.

We hadn't heard much from the half Fae man other than letting us know that Grey was fine. He'd been locked in solitary for a day because of a fight with a shifter, but other than that, they were all okay.

"He might, but that's not something I can ask over the phone or via text. He's too careful to let them figure anything out, but they could trace the call to me. Not to mention he's searched randomly, including his phone. The Fae don't trust him."

"Because he's a half breed." I snarled.

"Exactly. They weren't exactly kind when they found out a half Fae was already a guard in that prison when they took over but let him stay."

"Figure out how you can get word to him and pick the teams. We'll come up with a better plan then blow shit up and ask questions later." I cocked a brow at Ash, but he just chuckled.

"It's a solid plan," Ash defended himself with a scoff. "And if we take out a few Fae fucks in the process, I'm not gonna be mad."

He wasn't wrong there. I didn't care what we did as long as it got us to Grey and the others. Every day they sat in there was a day too long as far as I was concerned.

We needed to get them out, or I was afraid what Ronaldo and the other Fae might do to them. I would kill them all and laugh while doing it if anything happened to Grey and my friends.

CHAPTER 14

GREY

I shot up from the cot when the electronic buzzing of the door sounded in my cell. Two guards threw Fenrick's unconscious body on the concrete floor.

He was a mess of bruises and bloody cuts all over his chest, the word *traitor* etched in his skin and still bleeding.

"Fuck! What did he do to you?" I raced to him.

Blood was flowing out of his wounds far too quickly for my liking. It didn't appear to be stopping. I howled in anguish when all I could find in the cell was my wadded-up shirt.

"Grey? What is it?" the shifter in the cell next to ours asked as more howls filled the cell block.

"They fucking tortured him and the bleeding isn't stopping. I need something to stop the flow, but all I have is my shirt," I growled.

I held my shirt to the worst of his wounds, but it quickly soaked in too much blood. I could barely recognize Fenrick's bruised and beaten face.

His lips were split on both sides of his mouth and his eyes were black and swollen shut.

"Here!" The shifter called out and handed a piece of cloth around the bars. "There's more coming."

"What do you mean, more?" I asked.

"All the shifters in the block are tearing their shirts and whatever they can find to help him," the shifter said.

I grabbed the cloth from him and quickly wrapped it around the worst wound on his side. It was cut open with a blade, like Ronaldo was personally offended by Fenrick. Maybe he was. Ronaldo thought all Fae should be loyal to him and the Council.

More and more pieces of shirts and sheets came around the bars until I had all the bleeding wounds tied off.

"Do you all see what I mean now? None of us in this place are safe from whatever whims Ronaldo has. He can torture or kill us at any time, and there is nothing we can do to stop it!" I yelled for the entire cell block to hear.

"We have to get out of here," someone whispered. "We have to fight back."

"Yes, but we have to be smart about it. We can't just fight back without a plan."

I wanted them all to know that we were getting out but not to go crazy and get themselves thrown in the hole or tortured in here. We had to play along for now.

I sat with my arms around my knees as I watched Fenrick's steady breathing. At least he was breathing normally now, and the flow of blood was slowing.

"Blood, death," Fenrick muttered in his sleep.

Shit. What the fuck was he dreaming about that those

words would come out in his sleep? It was a little too ominous for my liking.

A whimper from the cell next to mine met my ears. "Is he awake? Did he hear something when he was being tortured?"

"No, he's still out cold. I don't know why he said that. It could be a trauma response to the torture. We won't know until he wakes up."

I checked his wounds again and redressed them but they seemed to be healing. Fenrick was Fae, so at least his healing abilities were working better for him than mine had.

"Days..." Fenrick groaned.

I couldn't tell if he was waking up or still dreaming because his eyes were still swollen shut. He gripped my arm to pull me closer to him.

"Fenrick? Holy shit. Are you okay?"

I didn't know what I was thinking. Of course, he wasn't okay. He looked like he was put through a meat grinder.

"Grey, murdered," he mumbled.

"No, I'm right here." I clutched his hand.

It was about the only place on his body that wasn't beaten or bloody.

"What's going on?" the other shifter asked.

"I think he's waking up but he's not coherent. He said something about me being murdered."

"Three days." Fenrick groaned.

He cracked an eye open, but his pupil was blown wide. Did he have a concussion? Probably.

"What about three days?" I asked. confused.

"Death, blood," he said then passed back out.

"I don't know if I'm understanding him correctly but whatever he's saying doesn't sound like it's going to end well for us."

Whimpers and growls from the other shifters in the cell block filled the air, and I couldn't exactly blame them. I rested my head back against the wall, my arms propped up on my knees as I waited for Fenrick to wake the fuck up.

A hand nudged me, and my eyes shot open. I must have dozed off because Fenrick was blinking his eyes at me. The swelling had lessened enough for him to see.

I shot to my feet and gently pulled him into a sitting position, but he still winced.

"What happened?" I asked. "You were mumbling about three days and death and blood."

"Fuck!" Fenrick shouted and jumped to his feet, but stumbled and nearly crashed back to the floor.

"Gods, Fenrick, take it easy. You lost a ton of blood." I steadied him and sat him down on the cot.

"You don't understand. We have to get out of here. Everyone is going to die." He turned to me wide-eyed.

"Are you sure you don't have a concussion?" I asked.

"I overheard some of the guards talking about moving people to the testing facilities. They were saying they couldn't wait until this place was rubble." Fenrick gripped my arm.

"Are you sure? You may have heard wrong. You were pretty beat up when they dropped you in here." I sat next to him.

"I know what I heard, Grey. They left me in there for dead, thinking I wouldn't make it so there was no point being quiet around me. They planned for me to die in front of you." He ran a hand through his hair and winced.

"Fucking hell. Tell me everything," I growled.

"The plan was never to make us their slaves but to test on anyone that could be useful to their plans and eradicate the rest." He hung his head.

"Test us for what? What are they trying to do? I never thought the facilities were for the Fae but for the humans. I thought that was part of the agreement. The Council hands over some of their slaves to the humans for testing, and they could do what they wanted. What am I missing?" I leaned forward with my elbows on my knees.

"The Council has been using human technology to create bio weapons to use against all who oppose them." Fenrick moved to jump up again, but I put a hand on his shoulder.

"What kind of bio weapons are we talking?" I asked.

"For one thing, they developed a mind control serum. Fae can read minds, but the scale they want to control people on is terrifying."

"That's what the testing facilities are doing." I shook my head.

"They let a lot of information out in front of me they probably shouldn't have, but like I said, they don't expect me to ever leave here alive." Fenrick grimaced.

"What else could there possibly be?" I asked, not exactly sure if I really wanted to know.

What he'd already said was terrifying enough.

"I guess shifters are resistant to the serum, and they have no clue why." Fenrick rubbed his eyes.

"So the shifters are being taken in for testing," I mused. "What about the rubble comment?"

"In three days, everyone in this place is going to be cannon fodder. They're going to kill us all."

"Fuck. That's not enough time." I ran a hand through my hair.

"How the hell are we going to plan and execute a prison break in three days?"

"We have people to help now, but it's still going to be a stretch," I said. "But we need to find a way to get these damn cuffs off."

"Grey?" the shifter in the next cell whispered low.

"What is it?" I asked.

"We might be able to get close to a guard. My cell mate is an accomplished pickpocket."

"That's a good start," I agreed. "As long as he doesn't get caught and thrown in the hole."

"Who are you talking to?" Fenrick asked with a frown.

"A lot happened while they were torturing you. A bunch of shifters have requested protection. That's how I got the stuff to dress your wounds."

"What did he say?" Fenrick asked.

Boots stomped down the hall along the cell block, and I grimaced. "Later."

The guard who'd been helping us stepped into view and my shoulders relaxed.

"They expected you to die in this cell." He nodded to Fenrick.

"I'm stronger than I look." Fenrick shrugged.

The guard swiped his badge on the scanner and the door opened. "I'm here to take you to the showers. You need new clothes before you go to the mess hall. You both do, apparently."

We followed him out of the cell and down a hall I hadn't

been in before. A huge communal shower stood at the end of the hall.

"You have five minutes to get cleaned up. There are new clothes in the lockers over there." He pointed to a bank of lockers and then turned his back on us.

Fenrick's body was stiff as he moved to unravel the makeshift bandages on his chest. I turned away, not willing to waste a minute of the short time we were given for the shower.

"So, what did the shifter say?" Fenrick muttered beneath his breath as the roar of water from the shower filled the air.

"His cellmate can get us a key." I held my arm up to show my cuff.

His eyes widened. "That's pretty useful."

"Yeah, but will it be enough?" I scrubbed my hair and tilted my head beneath the spray of the shower.

"It's a start, but if it's only shifters against the guards, we don't stand a chance."

"I have an understanding with the warlocks but I'm not bringing them in on the plan when we make it, just telling them to be ready." The guard didn't give us any soap or anything to wash with so I scrubbed as best as I could with my hands.

I wasn't clean but I felt at least a bit refreshed. The water ran cold, so I turned it off and headed to the lockers the guard had indicated.

The shirts and pants in there all looked the same, only different sizes, and I grabbed a set in my size and pulled them on when Fenrick walked up beside me.

"What are the odds we can come across some of the guards' uniforms and get out that way?"

I glanced down at my own bulk and then raised an eyebrow

at him. Fae were naturally lean and tall. There wasn't a guard in the place whose uniform would fit me.

"Even if we could, it wouldn't work. The shifters are all too large to fit in those uniforms." I shook my head.

"Let's go!" the guard yelled.

I was really getting tired of being ordered around. It was against my nature to let people boss me around and I'd had enough.

We trudged back to the guard, but he didn't move, peering down the hall to make sure we were alone. "You have two days to get yourselves and the shifters out of here. They are moving all the shifters to the testing facility before this place is taken out. They want you specifically, Grey. You need to get out."

"I know, Fenrick overheard them." I crossed my arms over my chest.

"Fuck," Fenrick cursed. "That moves the timeline up and we still don't have a plan."

"We'll do whatever it takes to stop this from happening. They want me alive as the king of the shifters. But I won't go down without a fight.

We would get out of this or die trying. I didn't want to think about which option was more likely. Death was coming, and I had a feeling none of us would come out of this unscathed.

CHAPTER 15

AURELIA

"Where are they?" I asked for the thousandth time as I paced the empty parking lot.

Dan huffed. "They'll be here."

"It was hard enough to commandeer a prison van, but now the guy tasked with bringing it to us with enough explosives to level this place was missing.

"What if they were caught? Our entire plan hinges on us getting that van past security." I clenched my fists at my sides.

Ash patted my shoulder. "Let's not put that kind of thing into the universe."

Zeke stepped up on my other side with a smirk. "It will work out, Princess. Don't worry."

"What are you up to?" I asked with narrowed eyes.

"Why would you think I was up to something?"

"Because you're smirking at me like this is all part of the plan, and this is definitely not a part of the plan that I was involved in. Smash and grab, remember?"

"I remember." He grinned at me again.

"Ash, why is he doing that?" I asked.

"You're adorable when you're wound like a top." Ash chuckled.

"So not helping," I said.

The rest of the teams walked up to us, then looked confused by the lack of a transport van. Yeah, I was confused too. We only had one shot at this, and it was getting blown to smithereens.

"Stop fidgeting," Dan whispered. "They'll be here."

"Are you sure? Because they should have been here already."

"Maybe they got stuck in traffic?" Dan asked, but even he didn't seem so confident anymore.

"Close ranks, we may have a problem," Ash said as he peered at something over my shoulder.

I spun around and gasped as sirens blared and several black prison vans sped up the street. "Shit. Someone betrayed us."

"Be calm. Fight them but in the end surrender," Zeke muttered under his breath.

I turned, glaring at the rider of the hunt. "What did you do?"

"I got us in the prison under our terms and without bloodshed." Zeke shrugged.

"Can I kill him?" I turned to Ash with magic lighting my palms.

"Not today, Princess. Not until we know the plan." Ash pushed his brother.

Zeke stepped back and raised his hands. "Just follow my

lead. We needed to get in and I'm getting us in. We don't have much time before they eradicate everyone in the place."

"What?" I shrieked as the vans drew closer. "You could have started with that instead of going behind our backs and coming up with your own plan."

Could I get away with smacking a rider of the wild hunt? I sure hoped so, because even though I really liked Zeke, I liked being informed when there was a change in plans even more.

"All the shifters are being moved to the testing sites and everyone else is going to blow up in an explosion, which is set to go off in three days."

"Why did that change the plan, though?" Asher growled.

"Because they will be expecting a simple smash and grab. Follow my lead." Zeke glared at Ash.

"Fine. What happens when they see me and realize who I am?" I asked.

The vans were almost on us and I really wanted to punch Zeke but he wasn't wrong. They would probably be expecting someone to try to break in.

"You will most likely be taken to the medical unit. Use that to your advantage," Zeke mumbled.

The vans surrounded us, and my magic thrummed beneath my skin. Shadows pulsed with excitement at the thrill of the fight.

Guards flooded out of the vans like a swarm of ants with guns raised. I flicked my wrist and magic and shadows mixed and blasted through several guards. I didn't care about Zeke's bullshit plan. I wasn't going to make it easy on them.

"Princess, behind you!" Ash shouted.

I spun on my heel and blasted the group of guards raising

their guns at me. They flew back into one of the vans with a thud.

"They just keep coming," I growled.

Arms wrapped around me from behind, and I flipped the man over my shoulder and flicked my wrist, sending him skidding to the others where his head smacked into a hubcap.

"Take her alive!" one of the guards yelled pointing at me.

"Shit," I said, spinning to Zeke with a glare. "There are too many of them."

Three guards rushed me, but Ash and Zeke got to them first, leveling them with a powerful blast of magic. The ground rumbled beneath my feet, and everyone but me stumbled to the side. My magic buzzed beneath my skin angrily.

Was I doing that? The ground beneath one of the vans split in a wide chasm and it crashed inside, exploding in a fiery ball of flames.

"Aurelia, tone it down!" Ash yelled. "You're taking out ours along with theirs."

I heaved in a breath and did my best to control the magic pulsing from me, but it wouldn't stop. The strength was overwhelming that came out to protect me from the threats.

"I'm trying!" I screamed as another chasm opened beneath two guards who were racing toward me. It swallowed them up and closed over their heads.

But still more guards flooded the once empty parking lot. Where were they all coming from? It didn't make any sense until I scanned the area and glanced at the man who ordered them to take me. He had a phone in his hand and was talking to someone.

"Take him out," I said, pointing. "He's calling for back-up."

I took deep, controlled breaths and finally the ground stopped shaking. Several of my team went after the leader. I spun around as a grunt sounded behind me. Dan stood there with a gun in his hand and a guard knocked out on the ground.

"Keep your eyes open, Princess. The cowards keep trying to sneak up behind you." Dan said and fired the gun in his hand.

He had my back, which would have surprised me before, but he was loyal to Grey and that made him loyal to me as well.

"Enough. You're surrounded. Surrender now!" the lead guard bellowed.

It went against everything inside me to surrender. I glanced at Zeke warily. *He better know what he's doing.*

I nodded imperceptibly to Zeke and Dan, and they ordered everyone to stand down. "If I get tortured again, I'm going to kick your ass."

"Trust me," Zeke whispered as we were swarmed.

Three guards grabbed my arms, clamping cuffs on my wrists behind my back. The leader sauntered up to me with a grin.

"I'm going to be rewarded for bringing you in." He ran his index finger down my cheek, and I snapped my teeth at him as Ash and Dan struggled against the guards that were holding them.

"Don't fucking touch her!" Ash bellowed.

His power glowed in his eyes as he raged against the guards.

"You don't have the power here, criminal. Your cuffs block your magic." The man grinned.

"Please don't evil villain monologue," I groaned.

"You're feisty. Maybe the High Councilor will let me play with you." The leader's eyes glittered with lust.

All the guys struggled against their bonds, trying to get to me or tear him to shreds. I wasn't sure which was more likely, but probably the latter.

I shook my head, accepting my fate. I would see Ronaldo in this prison, and he'd probably torture me again before he killed me, but at least the others would get Grey and everyone else out before the whole damn place blew.

I stared Zeke down as the leader yanked on my arm to move me to one of the transport vans.

His plan had better be a good one, or he was in some serious shit. Anger pulsed within me, and shadows curled around my fingers lazily just so I knew it was there.

Wait. I have my magic?

I snapped my gaze back to Zeke and he shook his head, eyes wide as he stared at my fingers. How did I have my magic? Those cuffs were supposed to block it. Do they just not work on me? Either way, I needed to hide it, or they would find another way to block my magic. I banished the shadows quickly before anyone saw, and raised my brows at Zeke.

Was this part of the amazing plan he didn't tell us about, or was this another way I was different from everyone else?

The back door to the van opened to two bench seats one on each side. There were no windows. The van had practically been gutted. The guard yanked me up into the van in front of him and pushed me forward. I fell heavily on the seat at the end closest to the front panel.

The leader sat down next to me with a leer, and my skin crawled as he rested a hand on my thigh. There was nothing I could do with my hands behind my back, and he knew it.

Asher was shoved in and sat in front of me. He lunged forward to get in the leader's face but was hit in the back of the head with the butt of the gun in the guard's hands that sat down next to him.

"You will behave as a prisoner should, or we will not be lenient!" the leader barked.

"Get your filthy, fucking paws off the princess, traitor," Ash gritted out between his clenched teeth.

"Again, you don't make demands here. You're my prisoner as she is, and I can do as I please." His hand inched up my thigh even more.

Dan eyed the hand like he could cut it off with only his mind, but I shook my head at them. I didn't want them getting knocked out or worse because the Fae bastard was getting handsy.

The leader squeezed my thigh so hard I would have bruises later, and I flinched away, practically plastering myself to the wall to get away from him. I needed to stay calm and not telegraph the fact that I still had access to my magic.

It was going to be difficult if the man kept putting his hands on me.

He fished his phone from his pocket and pressed a button. "We got twenty incoming and tell the High Councilor to meet me in medical. I come bearing gifts." He grinned, glancing at me through the corner of his eye.

Fuck. I knew he'd get Ronaldo in there right away to deal with me.

I stared at Zeke with both a warning and a threat in my eyes. The big bastard grinned at me. Yes, he'd been right about where I would be taken, but that wasn't a good thing.

Ronaldo wasn't going to let me out of his sight once he got

me in the medical unit. He wouldn't put me with everyone else. I wouldn't see Grey or ever find out what Zeke's plan was.

Damn. I wish I could read minds.

It fell silent in the van, none of us willing to give the guards a reason to punish us. I wasn't about to talk and possibly make the guards suspicious, either.

The road leading to the prison was bumpy, and I jostled around a lot but other than that, it was uneventful.

The tall, imposing building came into view and filled me with dread. We had to go in there. Now that I was seeing it, I realized our plan had been foolish. There was a brick wall surrounding the building and five guards at the gate waiting to check the identification of the guards and usher us through.

How had I ever thought we could pull that off? I hoped that Zeke's plan was better than mine because if not, we all might die in there.

CHAPTER 16

GREY

"Why would people try to break in?" a shifter whispered.

"What?" I asked through the bars.

Fenrick raised a brow at me.

"A large group was brought in last night. The rumor is they tried to break into the prison but were betrayed and caught," the shifter said louder this time.

"Fuck, you don't think?" Fenrick asked.

"That it wasn't a break-in, but a rescue mission? Yeah that's exactly what I think." I covered my face with both hands.

"Who do you think it was?" Fenrick asked.

"My money is on Dan and the Syndicate, but I wouldn't put it past the riders of the hunt to do something like that as well." I peeked between my fingers at him.

That was monumentally stupid of them to try to break into the prison like that. If it was them, then who is running the Syndicate?

"How many?" I asked the shifter.

"I don't know exactly, just that the group was big. Around twenty, I think."

"If it's who I'm thinking, they probably left the damn place unguarded. Damn it." I jumped to my feet and paced the length of the cell.

If this was Dan, then we were in deeper than we thought.

"Easy, Grey," Fenrick said. "We already planned to get everyone out and if it is your guys, at least they are well trained to assist us in escaping."

He was right, but it still left me uneasy. They weren't supposed to come after me if I ever got caught. Who could have convinced them to perform an extraction like that?

Growling at the end of the cell block caught my attention just before a set of boots stomped down the hall toward us.

I spun to the door and waited for the guard that usually helped us with my hands on my hips. It wasn't him. A different guard stood by the door and sneered at us.

"Where's my usual guard?" I asked.

"Shut up, mutt!" the guard barked, opening the door with his badge.

I glanced at Fenrick, dread pooling in my gut. Did we get him killed?

"Let's go. I don't want to wait around all day to escort filth to the mess hall!" the guard roared.

We stalked out of the cell together, shoulder to shoulder as we followed the asshole guard to the mess hall in tense silence.

Who were these new prisoners and why would the guards take them there if they were just going to level the place in two days? I had so many questions my mind spun, and my brain ached.

We pushed through the doors to the mess hall and got in line. I scanned the faces of everyone in the room and my gaze landed on turquoise eyes. "Fuck."

Fenrick spun in the direction of the riders of the hunt. "Well, that answers that question."

We grabbed our food and made our way to the table in the back. Magna and the king sat with Asher and Zeke, along with their brothers.

"What the fuck, Ash?" I dropped my tray on the table with a glare.

"What can I say? It all got fucked up." Ash waved his hands.

"I would say it all got fucked up if you're sitting across from me in this hell." I shook my head.

"It didn't all get fucked up," Zeke grumbled.

"You fucked us all over," Dan said.

"I'm telling you that it's better this way," Zeke growled.

"Yeah, better eating fucking gruel and waiting for the hammer to drop on our heads. So much better." Dan clenched a fist around his fork.

I glanced between the men that were all glaring at Zeke. What the fuck did he do? He was the reason they were all there, I was sure. Dread sank into my stomach like a stone. Who was here and what was happening at the Syndicate with everyone in prison?

I sat heavily on the bench. "Who else is here?"

"Dan brought in three teams along with us and your mate," Ash said slowly.

"Aurelia is here?" I asked scanning the mess hall to no avail. "Where the fuck is she?"

Relief that she survived the fall filled me but was quickly squashed when I processed what he'd said. She was in the prison. She'd tried to break in and rescue us and was caught. She was too close to Ronaldo's sadistic ass for my liking being locked up in here.

"They immediately separated her from us, and we haven't seen her since." Zeke shook his head.

Fuck. My mate is alive but hidden somewhere in this gods forsaken hellhole?

"You never should have brought her here," I growled.

"Right. Like she would let us leave her behind," Zeke scoffed.

He wasn't wrong. They would have had to lock her in a cell to get her to stay behind. So either way, she would have been locked away.

"Fine, I get it. She never would have stopped." I didn't like it, but I understood why they'd brought her along.

"What's going on outside?" I asked.

We got zero information locked away.

"The human government is rounding up all suspected supernaturals for testing and making them register as a supernatural." Ash clenched his fist around his roll and turned it to dust.

"It's all bullshit." I picked up my fork and stabbed the mushy substance that passed off as food.

"What do you mean?" Ash frowned.

"They are out to execute everyone who isn't useful. That's why I'm so freaked out about Aurelia being here. The prison is gonna blow in two days, and sometime tomorrow they are moving all the shifters so they can test their mind control serum on us."

Zeke shook his head. "I knew that they were going to blow the place up, but I thought it was to kill off all the royalty from Faery so they couldn't be challenged."

"Nope. As the Shifter King, I'm prime testing material." I grimaced and shoveled food into my mouth and swallowed without tasting it.

"We all need to get out of here. Ronaldo is probably coming in his pants with excitement having us all locked away in here." Ash wiped the crumbs from his hand and grabbed the roll from my tray, tearing into it with his teeth.

A shifter reached over and handed me his roll. Zeke raised a brow at that but didn't comment. The other shifters were constantly giving me gifts for protection. All I did was tell some warlocks to back off.

Zeke drummed his fingers on the table. "So we need to get out of here tonight?"

"That would be ideal, but we don't have a way." I glanced at Dan. "Your man disappeared. They gave us a new guard this morning."

"Fuck. Was he made?" Dan asked and rubbed a hand down his face.

"I don't know." I sighed.

"This isn't good. I was hoping that we had him on the inside at least." Dan hung his head.

"Don't worry." Zeke patted Dan's shoulder. "It doesn't change the plan."

"The plan you refuse to share with the class," Dan grumbled.

I snapped my gaze to Zeke. What the fuck did he do? The rider shook his head and smirked.

Magna placed a hand on my arm. "Don't. This is for the best."

"What did you see?" I asked.

"You know I can't tell you that." She shook her head.

"I know, but I hate being the last to know the plan." I tilted my head back, squeezing my eyes shut.

"Your shifter is coming," Magna said. "He has something for you."

I turned just as the shifter that worked for the Syndicate bounded up to me. He had a grin on his face and reached into his pocket. I growled like a rabid beast.

"Later. If that's what I think it is, the guards are always watching me here," I whispered so low only a shifter could hear.

His eyes widened and his gaze flicked around the room noting all eyes on us. Especially since we were currently sitting with the supernaturals who'd tried to break in.

"No problem, boss." He nodded then glanced at Dan. "Shit. What are you doing here?"

"We were framed. They thought we were breaking into the prison for some unknown reason, and they brought us in," Dan lied easily.

"You really think I believe that?" The shifter raised a brow at Dan.

"I don't care what you believe. We have eyes on us and that's the only thing I'm telling you." Dan stared the shifter down and he bowed his head in submission.

"Sit down," I said to the shifter pointing at a spot next to the Shadow King.

He'd been uncharacteristically silent after the news that Aurelia was in this hellhole with us and probably worried that she was in the hands of Ronaldo. I was just as worried but needed this information to help us all. We had to get everyone out of here and we needed to do it sooner rather than later.

I glanced over my shoulder at the guard who'd replaced the one that helped me. His eyes gleamed with malice. He was going to be a tough one to get past. He may not make it out of the prison, and I wasn't sure that I gave a fuck because he was definitely drinking the Council's Kool-aid.

I glanced at the shifter as he sat next to the Shadow King and then back at Zeke. "We only have one shot at this. Are you going to be ready to go tonight? And how do we get Aurelia out?"

Magna nudged my shoulder. "We are ready and able to get out tonight. Your shifter has what you need, and your mate will be ready. Trust me."

I did trust Magna. Her visions had never failed me. She always seemed to point me in the right direction even if she couldn't tell me everything I needed to know. A lot of the time it was better for her to keep things close to her chest.

We didn't want to change the outcome of Fate if she was pointing us in the right direction.

"Okay, I get it. I'll play along." I glared at him. "I don't like being left in the dark, Zeke. And I hate that my mate is probably being tortured right now."

"I know but we can't just talk about this out in the open.

You never know who might be listening." Zeke scanned the room.

"Shifter hearing would be an issue if all the shifters here weren't loyal to me."

"Loyalty can be bought with freedom. Though it would be a lie and we all know it." Zeke clenched his fist on the table.

"Anyone who betrays us in this place can rot," I said loud enough for all to hear.

"That was subtle." Ash smirked.

"They need to know what the stakes are here. They need to know that there will be no mercy for betrayal." I shrugged.

"Well, you are definitely giving off *I'm gonna kill you* vibes, so there's that." Zeke chuckled.

Something shoved me in the back, and I turned to the guard behind me. He sneered at me.

"Time to go, mutt." The guard poked me in the back with his baton.

I nodded to the others and stood from my seat with Fenrick at my side. I still didn't know what the plan was, but it seemed neither did anyone else.

Zeke was keeping it quiet. I would be ready, though. I didn't have a choice, because if I wasn't ready for anything, then whatever plan Zeke was hatching would end in death.

CHAPTER 17

AURELIA

"Stay in here." The leader shoved me into a sterile white operating room.

The click of the lock as he closed the door was like a gunshot to my ears. I was going to kill Zeke for this. Damn rider was a pain in my ass.

The only thing in the room was an operating table and there were no windows. What the hell did Ronaldo use this room for? Had he been torturing my people? My only saving grace was that Dan's man on the inside told him that they were still alive. If it weren't for that knowledge, I would have already lost control.

I paced the small room, wringing my hands together. This was stupid. Why had I let them take me instead of fighting harder? My hands shook, and I wiped the sweat from my palms on my jeans.

Something buzzed before the door was pushed open and Ronaldo stood there with a smug grin on his face and several guards flanking him. "Princess."

"Ronaldo," I said with a sneer. "You won't get away with all of this."

"But I already have, Princess. You have no one left and after tomorrow, you will all be dead or under my control."

He snapped at the guards, and they advanced on me. I struggled slightly but let them strap me to the operating table. I couldn't let him know that I still had my magic. I still had no idea what Zeke's plan was, but I knew that it wasn't underway yet and I needed to bide my time.

"You think you can control me?" I scoffed.

"I will have no problem controlling you, girl. You are nothing but a nuisance." He took a threatening step toward me.

"Then why are you so obsessed with me?" I laughed.

The Councilman had a sick obsession with hurting and controlling me and though I did kind of get the reasons behind it, there was so much about the prophecy that I didn't know.

"You are in my way. You are the only one who can end this before it begins but not anymore. Now I have you exactly where I want you, and you won't be getting away again." Chills rolled down my spine at Ronaldo's evil grin.

"You're sick and twisted. If you hadn't turned the Fae against the supernaturals in the first place, there would be no need of a prophecy. You were drunk on the power and wanted more. You want to rule humans, which is stupid since they outnumber us by a great deal."

"I tire of your mouth. Maybe when I have you under my control, I will give you to Malcolm. He has always had a soft spot for his *betrothed*."

Real terror snaked in my chest and my stomach plummeted.

He couldn't really control the minds of Fae, right? Fae had shields. They shouldn't be able to be controlled?

Ronaldo wheeled a cart in with medical tools, and I flinched. Was he going to torture me so I would drop my shields? How long could I hold out against his torture without using my magic?

"You can't control me," I said through gritted teeth.

Ronaldo's sadistic laugh filled the small space as he picked up a syringe and gripped my arm. Magic tingled beneath my skin, but I held it back. I refused to show signs that I had my magic.

It would be catastrophic.

He pushed the syringe in my arm and the cool liquid plunged into my veins, leaving an icy chill in its wake. The tingling of foreign magic in my veins started at my arm and arched up through my body to my head.

"In just a few seconds you will be completely under my control." Ronaldo grinned.

My magic battled with whatever he'd just injected me with, and I shivered. Whatever the substance was, it was powerful. My back arched as my magic turned molten in my veins and Ronaldo dropped the grin on his face as my entire body started shaking.

"What is happening?" Ronaldo asked, taking a step forward and leaning over me. "She shouldn't be able to fight it off. It should be working already."

One of the guards stepped forward. "She's powerful. Maybe the magic blocking-cuffs only work so she can't use magic outside her own body?"

I held back a scream as my magic boiled me from the inside.

It was excruciating, but whatever drug Ronaldo had used on me was burned up within seconds and I slumped back down on the operating table with relief.

It was short lived, though.

"Get me more!" Ronaldo barked at a guard. "Double the dose. She can't fight it off forever."

"Sir, that much could kill her," the leader that brought me in said. "You promised I could play with her once she was under your control."

"Well, she won't be under my control until we can stop her magic from fighting the serum, will she?" Ronaldo yelled.

He was really going to do this. My shadows tried desperately to free themselves and protect me from the threats in the room. I held them off as best as I could, unwilling to show my hand just yet.

"If she dies she will be of no use either, sir." The leader crossed his arms over his chest.

"She's good for nothing but to please my men. She's already been sentenced to death for crimes against Faery. What do I care if the princess dies. Everyone who would care is in a cell and will be joining her in death soon enough."

I gasped at his words. It hadn't been real until I heard it from his lips. He really was out to destroy all supernaturals. He never had a plan to enslave them but rather destroy them.

"If you're planning on killing us all, why bother experimenting on us?" I asked.

"The humans believe they're in control and required testing facilities to learn more about us. They are particularly stupid. The mind control is a failsafe for any who manage to avoid capture and death." Ronaldo shrugged.

The other guard rushed back into the room with a tray in his hands. The syringe was even bigger on that tray. Electric blue liquid sloshed in the syringe, and I yanked at my arms trying to get free. My magic had a mind of its own when it came to protecting me from that crazy shit and it hurt like a bitch.

I clenched my fists and tugged on the straps, but they were so tight I wasn't getting anywhere. Ronaldo clamped a hand down on my arm and held me still as he brought the syringe down on my arm.

My magic swirled within me, and shadows danced behind my eyes as I screamed in pain. My magic heated up and became an inferno in my body, trying to burn away the much larger dose. Convulsions wracked my body, and I had no idea how I managed to keep my magic under control.

It pulsed inside of me, burning away the toxin and the convulsions eased, allowing me to slump back on the table in relief.

"No!" Ronaldo roared.

He squeezed my arm harder as he raged. I closed my eyes and did my best to calm my magic that was waging war inside me, dying to get out.

He pulled the cart full of implements closer to him and a crazed grin tipped up his lips. He was going to torture me.

"How are you doing that?" Ronaldo growled. "That large of a dose would have killed a grown man and you are a small slip of a girl."

"Fuck you," I sneered.

I didn't care. He could torture me all he wanted. The wounds would heal probably faster than he would expect, and then I would get the fuck out of there at my first opportunity.

He grabbed a scalpel and held it up for me to see. "I carved the words *shifter scum* into your shifter with this scalpel. It's only fitting that I use it to carve into your pretty flesh as well."

The gleam in his eyes would have scared the piss out of a grown-ass man, but I knew what was coming. He'd done this to me before and I refused to take the bait. It wasn't shocking that the sadist had tortured Grey.

"Doesn't matter what you do, I'm still going to be your end." I smirked.

"The traitor screamed so beautifully for me as I practically bled him dry. He wasn't supposed to make it out of here alive. I have your shifter to blame for that. Oh, well, there will be plenty of time to torture him at the testing facility."

He planned to send Grey to the testing facility? He wasn't going to kill him here like the rest of us? That would destroy Grey more than any torture possibly could.

No. I couldn't think like that. We were all getting out of here and then taking the Council down once and for all.

The scalpel scraped down my arm as Ronaldo dug it as deep as he could into my skin. Fire burned in my veins as blood trickled down my arm and pooled on the table beneath me. I locked my jaw against a groan of pain.

The worst part though, was the expression of euphoria on the High Councilor's face. He was getting off on torturing me. If that wasn't just sick and twisted, I didn't know what was.

"Tell me how you keep burning through my influence, and this all stops. I'll take you to a cell where you can heal until the explosion."

"Fuck off." I gritted out.

He slashed at my arm, cutting across the other cut in an X. I squeezed my eyes shut and held back my whimper of agony.

My skin burned with pain even as my magic jumped to heal my injuries. It was the only thing I would allow it to do as I kept it in a strangle-hold.

This was the exact place Zeke wanted me to go, and I needed to figure out why before they put the plan into action. I just had no idea how to do that with Ronaldo slicing me up. He moved from my arm and the scalpel pressed into my cheek, but not hard enough to break the skin yet.

His angry gaze pinned me to the table. "How are you healing so quickly?"

"I don't know."

"Did someone tamper with her cuffs?" Ronaldo asked over his shoulder.

The leader stepped forward. "No, sir. I put those cuffs on her myself and no one has touched her since."

"I may have to keep you around at the testing facility after all if your magic is leaking through those cuffs." Ronaldo mused.

"With all due respect, sir. I don't think that would be wise. Even though subjects are strapped down they are less secure, and she could escape with the shifter."

Ronaldo dug the scalpel into my cheek and this time I did gasp at the pain so close to my eye. Hot blood trickled down my face to my lips, painting a bloody smile as I gathered some of my blood in my mouth and spit it in Ronaldo's face.

"You may be right. She's too wild to trust in the facility. She will just have to die with the rest of them." Ronaldo swiped the blood off his face and slashed at my cheek again.

He kept slashing at my face and arms until I did let out a

scream of agony. My back arched and blood drenched me and the table to which was strapped, but my magic got to work healing the worst of my injuries.

"I will be back for you, Princess. This time I will make sure you die like you should have in the Council chambers you destroyed."

"Fuck off, Ronaldo." I spit the words at him.

He was scum, but he held my life in his hands. How exactly did he plan to make sure I died this time? I wasn't sure and I really didn't want to find out.

CHAPTER 18

GREY

The electric buzzing of the door woke me, and I jumped to my feet, staring at Dan on the other side.

"How did you get out?" I asked as Fenrick and I moved to the door.

"Zeke is a smart bastard, let me tell you. He somehow planned it down to which cuffs they would put us in. He refused to tell us anything. Our cuffs are useless though. They don't block shit." He held out a hand to me.

I reached out and let him grip my wrist, turning it to place a small key in the hole and unlocking them. My wolf lunged to the surface as magic rushed through me in waves. I nearly stumbled.

Fenrick doubled over at the waist, probably feeling the same relief I had. I walked over to the cell next to mine and handed the shifter the key.

"Get this to everyone on the cell block. They all need to

unlock their cuffs," I said, turning back to Dan. "What's the plan?"

"Follow me." Dan took off down the hall that led to the showers, and I shrugged at Fenrick before jogging after him.

"Where are we going?" Fenrick asked.

"There's a control panel down this hall that will open all the cells in the prison. I need to get to it before anyone realizes we're out." Dan turned down a second hall.

Six guards stood around in a circle talking in hushed voices when we skidded around the corner. Fenrick blasted one with his magic as I rushed one, crouching low and taking him to the ground.

"Dan!" I shouted but he already had two others pinned to the ground with his magic.

I gripped the guard's baton and flicked the electricity on and hit him in the neck with it. He grunted before his eyes rolled in the back of his head.

I glanced up at the others, but they had already taken care of the other five guards.

"Let's go." Dan wiped his hands on his pants and turned down the hall.

Fenrick ran a hand down his face. "Are we stupid for leaving them alive? Is this going to come back to bite us?"

"It might, but they were just humans. Despite what they are doing to us right now, I don't like killing humans," I said.

"It won't matter in a minute," Dan called over his shoulder.

"Why is that?" I asked as he skidded to a stop in front of me.

"Because there are about to be a lot more of us than them." He grinned.

The black panel on the wall had a keypad on it keeping it

locked. Dan held a hand over it, and there was a loud pop and sparks flew from the keypad before the panel popped open.

"What are you doing?" I asked with a frown.

"Getting back-up." He flipped a switch and the lights flashed red as a siren sounded.

The cells all buzzed and grinding metal filled the hall. Dan whooped, fist pumping the air. We raced back to the cell block to see shifters stumbling out of their cells. Their cuffs no longer bound their animals.

Howls of excitement flooded the hall as they jumped all over each other. I grabbed the shifter that worked for me by the scruff of his neck.

"We aren't out of here yet. There are six guards in the back hall. They probably all have cuff keys. I need you to get them."

He nodded and grabbed another shifter, taking off in the direction I pointed. The rest of the shifters stopped celebrating and stood at attention, waiting for instructions. I turned to Dan with a raised brow.

"Do you know where the other supernaturals are being housed?"

"They are all in this block and the next block over, where they had me." He pointed down the hall.

"Good." I grabbed the shifter that was in the next cell. "Do you still have the keys?"

"Yes," he said.

"Go take the cuffs off the warlocks and others. I'll send help when they get back."

The shifter nodded and several took off to the next cell block to get the others out of their cuffs. Everyone needed full access to their magic.

"Where are the riders?" I asked Dan.

"They're holding off the guards until we can get everyone out of the cuffs."

I jogged down the hall and nearly ran into the shifters that were sent to get more keys. "Go help get the warlocks out of cuffs."

We raced to the end of the other block and past the warlock who'd been bullying the shifters before I came in. He nodded as he got his cuffs removed.

"What's the plan?" he asked.

"The plan is to get the hell out of here without dying." I shrugged.

I didn't even know what kind of plan Zeke had cooked up in that crazy head of his.

"That's not much of a plan."

"You're out of your cell and the cuffs, right?" I asked.

"Fair enough."

I stopped next to Ash and Zeke. "Okay, liar, how are we doing this?"

"That was harsh," Zeke said. "But not untrue."

"You can tell us the plan now, dipshit!" Ash barked.

"Someone is going to have to blast the doors open. We need Aurelia to get out of the medical unit before we can leave."

"We're sitting ducks right here. How long do you think we have before they call for back-up or try to blow this place early?" I asked, scrubbing a hand down my face.

"Probably only a few minutes," Zeke said.

"That's not exactly helpful." I sighed.

"We can hold them off." The warlock clapped me on the shoulder.

Magic lit his other palm and I grinned. It felt good to have all our powers back. I scanned the group of men all gathered around. We could do this. We could get out of here, but what were we going to do once we did?

"What was the state of the Syndicate when you left?"

"Overcrowded but fine. Why?" Zeke asked.

"We will need somewhere for everyone to go."

"That's what we've been doing this whole time. Gathering anyone who is outed as supernatural and giving them space at the building. We'll figure that out once we get there."

"Let's go, then." I jogged off to the other end of the cell block to the heavy metal door locking us all in.

Dan raced up with a badge in his hand and swiped it on the keypad. The alarm continued to blare in my oversensitive ears and the panel on the door flashed red.

"Fuck, it's not working." Dan grunted.

"Can you override it?" I asked, turning to Zeke.

He was the resident hacker. I'd never seen a system he couldn't break into. He had to be able to do something.

Zeke rushed to the panel on the door and typed a few things in but shook his head. "The override isn't working."

"Fuck." I slammed my hand on the door. "Can you get around it? What if you just blow the electronics inside like before?"

"I could try that, but I'm not sure if it will open or stay closed permanently." Dan leaned his forehead against the door.

He placed his palm on the scanner and magic lit his hand in a green glow. There was a pop of electricity and then nothing. The door didn't move. I shoved Dan out of the way and pushed the door, but it was too heavy for me to move on my own.

"Ash, Zeke, help me push this," I demanded.

The two riders and several others lined up on each side of me and we pushed the door. It creaked and groaned beneath our wait and force before finally sliding open. The supernaturals around us cheered as they flooded out of the main cell block to the front of the prison.

Guards flooded the place with their electric batons in their hands, barking orders that no one listened to. Shifters tore their clothes off and shifted quickly. Wolves and bears tore into guards all around me.

Blood sprayed me in the face as I rushed to help. My wolf prowled in my head, wanting out. It had been too long, but I had to hold back until we got out of this hell. The other shifters had no such thoughts, letting their animals tear through the guards without mercy.

I ducked as a guard swung his baton at my head. I punched him in the gut and all the air rushed from his lungs as he doubled over. I took the baton from him and bashed him in the head with it, knocking him out.

Something slammed into my back and arms circled my neck in a weak chokehold. I lunged forward, throwing the man over my shoulder, breaking his grip and slammed the baton into his skull.

"Grey, we're surrounded!" Ash yelled over the chaos.

He was also covered in blood that I was sure wasn't his. The shifters weren't taking prisoners.

"Shit." I spun around.

Eight guards were circling the two of us. Ash glared at the one standing in front of the rest.

"You want his death, brother." Ash clapped me on the shoulder and pointed at the man.

"Why is that?" I asked with a grin.

"He put his hands on your mate."

The grin slipped from my face. He did what now?

"I'll make it slow and painful then." I took a threatening step toward him with the baton twirling at my side.

"Yeah, that was me and once the High Councilor figures out how to control her, he's going to give her to me to play with." The man's eyes glowed with lust for my mate.

My wolf beat at the cage I had him locked in trying to take control. "I'm definitely going to kill you now."

With a hand motion, the entire group descended on us at once. We were overwhelmed and everyone else was in the middle of their own fights. If something didn't change quickly, we were royally screwed.

CHAPTER 19

AURELIA

I paced the small operating room when the lights flashed red, and an alarm blared in my ears. The door to the room swung open, hitting the wall behind it.

"What the hell are they doing?" I whispered to myself as I took tentative steps toward the door.

Chaos reigned outside as people in white lab coats scattered like ants. They raced for the doors I'd been brought through before muttering about getting locked in with the animals if they didn't hurry.

Of course, they think we are animals. Do they want to see what kind of animals we really can be?

My magic formed a ball in my hand. I threw my magic at cabinet, and it engulfed in flames. Several shrieks filled the room, and I rushed to the other tables, removing restraints from a man tied to a bed. He quickly got up, but he stumbled to the side. I steadied him but I needed to help the others before smoke filled the room.

"Go. I'll help," the man said and steadied himself on the bed.

"Okay." I nodded to the man and raced to the other beds.

Some were better off than others, but at least after a few seconds they could walk.

"Get to the main prison. I have something else I need to do." I spun back to the hell that the room I'd been tortured in was down and rushed through the medical unit, searching for the serum he'd used on me.

If I could destroy it, they wouldn't be able to use it on others. I had no idea if it was the only supply, but it would hurt the Council either way.

I glanced through the doors on both sides of the hallway, finding offices with computers. My magic swept through the room, frying every device in the office before moving on. Small pops of electricity followed in my wake.

Maybe I should have thought this through better. I'm going to have to come back this way.

I raced to the end of the hall and threw open the double doors using my magic. There was obviously a reason they didn't have that connected to the prison's evacuation system.

I stepped inside the room and growled low in my throat. It was a lab but there were people hooked to tubes and machines that were keeping them alive. What the fuck was I to do? I couldn't just leave them.

"Fuck!" I shouted.

"What is it?" A man's voice asked behind me and I spun, ready to throw magic until I recognized the man I helped before.

"I can't get them out of here. I don't even know if they're alive." I shook my head.

"I was an ER doctor before they started rounding us up." The man stepped forward.

There were two beds with people strapped to them and he got to work checking their vitals and muttered to himself. "Neither of them has any brain activity. I don't even know why they are keeping them alive."

"What the fuck?" I asked. "Why would they keep them alive without brain function?"

"The experiments they're doing here are pretty terrible. Maybe they want to be able to control something that doesn't have a free will to interfere."

"That's fucking terrifying. I think I would rather be dead than have my body used like a walking zombie." I shivered.

"They're gone. Light this place up before the fires spread and trap us back here." The man took a step back.

Magic flooded my system and I had to look at it as doing them a kindness as I let it fly at the shelf on the wall. There were vials of electric blue liquid there that had to be the same as the serum Ronaldo injected me with.

I could only hope that those were the only doses and the computer files I'd destroyed weren't backed up somewhere.

The glass vials exploded into vapor that filled the air and I coughed. "Get out of here. You might not be strong enough to fight it."

"What about you?" he asked, worried.

"I'll be fine. I've fought it off before. Go." I waved at him to hurry, and with one last unsure glance, he raced away.

Three more shelves were stocked with the blue liquid, and I

torched them all along with a couple of computers that dotted the room. A single tear tracked down my cheek as the machines keeping hearts beating popped with electricity and died.

Ronaldo and his Council were monsters testing on people, and I would make them pay for it.

I raced from the room as an explosion rattled the ground beneath my feet and made my way to the next room where there were shelves and shelves of the stuff. I let my magic go wild, glass shattering and raining down on the floor. Vapor hissed up into the ceiling and the vents in the walls.

Shit. I hope that doesn't affect the others' escape.

A ball of fire flew at me from my place in the doorway. I hurled myself to the side as the wall exploded. I rolled back to my feet and sprinted down the hall.

I think that's enough destruction for today. That should spread to the other rooms on its own. I don't need to add to the danger.

Were chemicals used in that room? That was a bit more of an explosion than I was ready to handle.

The entire medical unit sounded like a battlefield as electronics caught fire and chemicals exploded. I dodged several more fireballs as I directed my magic at the main room where the prisoners had been tested, frying the computers and any other vials of that foul serum as I raced away.

The ground rumbled beneath my feet as I rushed out the main door to the medical unit and slammed it behind me.

Gods, I hope no one else was in there. Those poor people were already dead, but please don't let anyone else be stuck in there.

I slammed my fist into the wall, furious that Ronaldo and

his Council were just using people for their own gain. I fucking hated it. The floor rolled beneath my feet as a deafening roar surrounded me. I pitched to the side and clutched at the wall.

I had to keep moving. I couldn't get caught up in the explosions or discovered by the Council's goons.

I picked my way through debris and burning embers as I shuffled through the hall to the main prison. That was the only part of the plan Zeke had told me. Meet at the front of the prison so we could get the fuck out of here.

He's probably not going to like the detour and chaos I caused. Oops. Oh, well. He can deal with it, considering that he did this to us, and I was tortured.

I rounded the corner and stopped dead in my tracks. Ronaldo stood in the hallway with a sneer on his face and two guards standing at attention at his back.

"What have you done?" Ronaldo roared.

I grinned. "My magic got a little angry at the atrocities happening here and blew some shit up."

He glanced down at the cuffs still on my wrists. "Impossible. You have the cuffs on. You can't possibly have your magic."

I called magic to my hands and Ronaldo's eyes widened.

"You were saying?" I smiled sweetly.

"How is that possible?" He turned furious eyes on his guards.

"I'm more powerful than whatever you have in these things." I shrugged.

"You are becoming more of a nuisance than I had ever imagined. Stop this, now."

"No," I growled, letting the magic build in my palms.

"I will kill you, Princess." Ronaldo took threatening a step forward.

"You've already threatened to do that many times." I smirked. "It's losing its effect on me."

"Insolent girl!" Ronaldo bellowed. "You could have been queen if you would have fallen in line with what we have planned."

"You mean keeping dead people alive for your own nefarious purposes? No fucking thank you." I shook my head and threw a ball of magic at the men.

They all dove out of the way and my magic blasted the wall behind them, shaking the building around me. The whole place was going to go up in flames soon. I needed to get out, but Ronaldo and his goons were still blocking my exit.

"Enough of this!" Ronaldo hollered. "I wanted to execute you publicly, but you are too much of a thorn in my side. Kill the princess."

The men with Ronaldo drew their guns, pointing them at my chest. Did he really think those were going to hurt me? Human weapons. I smirked.

"You are too cocky for your own good," I said.

"No, Princess, you are. Do you think mind control is the only weapon I have been working on?" Ronaldo chuckled. "That would have been very shortsighted of me, wouldn't it?"

"What are you talking about?" I asked.

I worried my lip at his smug expression and the flames licking up the walls all around us. I needed to get out of here, preferably without bullet holes in my chest.

"After we get rid of the supernaturals, the humans will

clearly be next. I couldn't have them possessing better weapons than us," Ronaldo scoffed.

I eyed the guns warily. What the fuck was in them? I didn't want to know.

"You made bullets that will kill us?" I gasped.

He was using human technology and mixing it with magic. It was a dangerous combination that would end disastrously if someone didn't stop him.

"We have many weapons now. More than you could ever imagine, but you won't live to see us use them on your rebellious friends."

"Rebellious? You're trying to eradicate them after exiling them for centuries. Why even come here and start this when you had Faery to yourself?" I threw my hands up.

"Because of you. Your birth signaled the end of that era, and we had to find a way to keep what we had."

I took a step back when he moved closer, not about to let him get his hands on me. The guards at his side cocked their weapons. Shit. What was I going to do now? I could use my magic, but what would the bullets in those guns do?

Was Ronaldo correct that they would kill me? Would they do something to my magic? I glanced around the hall again warily. Thick, black smoke rose into the air and flames danced along the walls.

The ground rumbled with another explosion, and I stumbled to the side. The guns followed me as I went.

"Kill her now, before the entire place comes down on our heads." Ronaldo commanded.

I was out of time. Ronaldo was about to have me killed and there wasn't anything I could do to stop it.

CHAPTER 20

GREY

"What the fuck?" I yelled as an explosion rumbled through the prison.

Had they decided to blow it up early?

We were still surrounded by guards. They wouldn't purposely blow up their own people, would they? Of course, they would. Ronaldo only cared about himself.

Several guards stopped advancing and glanced between each other, probably wondering the same thing.

The leader screamed, "Get them! The High Councilor wants the shifter alive."

The others still had wary expressions. They shuffled their feet and glanced at the door longingly. They were the smart ones, but they were torn between their duty and saving their own lives.

The other guards fled the room having the right idea. Some of the other supernaturals looked to me for guidance with the guards fleeing their fights they were free to run, and I didn't blame them if they did.

"Go," I said, waving them off.

I was outnumbered with just Ash and me up against eight of these assholes, but I didn't want anyone dying for me.

"No, stay and finish this!" the leader hollered as several men stepped toward the door.

"Is pleasing that jackass worth your life?" I asked. "This place is about to blow."

The men all took a step back except for the leader of the group. He stepped forward. "You're all cowards. I'll be rewarded when I bring you to the High Councilor."

"Wrong answer. Why do the bad guys always say stupid shit like that?" I asked, glancing at Ash.

"I think it's in the evil villain rule book that say they have to be morons." Ash rolled his shoulders back.

"Probably." I smirked.

"Who are you calling a moron, mutt? At least I was smart enough to choose the winning side." The leader grinned.

The men who had shown up with him were slowly backing toward the door because his attention was firmly on me. They were the smart ones. I would be getting the hell out of here the second I had my mate in my arms.

"You really think this looks like winning?" I waved my hand at the chaos around us.

Ash chuckled. "I mean, it looks like someone is winning, but not you."

He held up his baton threateningly. I dropped into a fighting stance now that it was a fair fight. My wolf howled in my head, desperate to be free. We needed to find Aurelia and get the hell out of here.

The man lunged with his baton, nearly catching me in the shoulder. I jumped back and crouched even lower.

"Is that all you've got?" I taunted.

I wasn't about to let him put one over on me. My wolf was seeing red. He wanted this idiot's blood.

Magic built in the man's palm as he lunged for me again. I dodged the ball of magic and it hit the wall with an ominous crack. It wasn't enough to do a ton of damage, but with the explosions wracking the prison, it was enough to be a concern.

"You're weak," I said.

His eyes flashed and glowed with hatred, but before he could throw more magic, he was swept off his feet on a gust of air. I glanced at Ash and grinned.

"You call me weak, but you can't even fight fair."

He swung again wildly, and I ducked below the baton and wrapped my arms around him, tackling him to the ground.

I gripped his wrist that held the baton and smashed it against the floor until he let it go and it rolled away. My hands shifted to claws as I wrapped them around his neck. They pierced the skin, blood gushing from him as he punched me in the kidney.

I grunted in pain but refused to let go. This man touched my mate and threatened to use her as a plaything. I was not going to stand for it. I promised many of the assholes in the place death, and his would be the first.

The man's skin paled as he clutched at my clawed hands. His blood soaked my skin. I'd nicked his carotid artery and he would bleed out within seconds. The last thing he saw would be my face. His end. His death.

"I told you, I would kill you for touching her," I said as the light went out of his eyes.

I retracted my claws back to my human hands and sat back on my haunches. One down. I scanned the room for any others who I made that promise to but didn't find them. The guards were fleeing from the explosion and in their haste left the doors wide open.

A hand was thrust into my view, and I took it, letting Ash pull me up. "That was pretty gruesome."

"Have you looked around? This whole scenario is pretty fucking gruesome." I wiped my bloody hands on my pants.

The roar of another explosion met my ears, and I spun in a circle, scanning the area for my mate when Dan jogged up to me.

"C'mon, Grey, we gotta run." Dan tugged at my arm to move.

"Where is Aurelia? I don't see her anywhere," I growled.

My wolf paced in my mind as I searched every face for her but came up empty. I turned to Zeke with a glare even as Dan tried again to nudge me to the door.

"We have to go before guards come back. I'm sure they will."

"They're blowing this place up early. The guards aren't coming back." I shook my head.

"That's not what this is. They would have just blown it up in one massive explosion. We have to go before they realize that and come back to find the cause." Dan ran a hand through his hair.

"I'm not leaving without my mate." I brushed his hand off my shoulder. "Where is she?"

"Medical unit," Zeke said.

"You all get out of here. Get everyone to the Syndicate. I have to go after Aurelia," I barked the orders.

I wouldn't have them all wait for me and die in the process. They needed to run because even if Dan was right and they didn't blow the place early, something was happening, and I had a sinking suspicion it was coming from the medical unit.

I turned on my heel and ran through the hall, not caring one bit for my own safety. Ash jogged up beside me and kept glancing over his shoulder warily.

"You got my back?" I asked.

Ash nodded. I turned the corner to the medical unit and flames licked up the walls.

What the hell happened here? Is my mate okay?

Thick, black smoke billowed through the hall. A chemical scent mixed with the smoke and a racking cough tore through me. Fuck. Did she blow up the lab?

Ash and soot covered the floor and I kept to the middle of the long hall, very aware that the walls were burning but I didn't care. I needed to find Aurelia and get us all out.

I refused to live in a world without her. I would follow her in death as well as life. She'd become everything to me, and I refused to fail her now.

I pushed through the main door that led to the unit and stopped in my tracks. Aurelia stood there, magic pooling in her palms as she faced off against Ronaldo and two guards who both had guns pointed at her chest. Flames grew ever closer to her by the second and the haze of smoke thickened in the air.

I lost control of my wolf as he lunged forward violently, completely taking me off guard. My wolf snarled at the men who turned wary eyes on me.

Ronaldo took a step back. "Kill the girl and get me the wolf, alive."

The men cocked their guns, taking aim at my mate, but Ash flicked his wrist, sending a gust of wind at them. The men stumbled to the side, and my wolf jumped in front of Aurelia, growling low and menacingly.

He wasn't about to let them get away. He could end this madness once and for all if he could just get to Ronaldo. My wolf stalked forward on silent paws, ready to rip their throats out for threatening his mate.

One of the men raised his gun to shoot me when Ronaldo hissed, "No, you fool. I need him alive."

Ronaldo's plans for domination really were more important to him than anyone doing his dirty work. My wolf lunged at the man, taking his wrist between sharp teeth and sinking them into his arm.

The man cried out as blood sprayed from his wrist. He dropped the gun on the floor, and I pushed it toward Ash with my paw.

"Careful," Aurelia said. "Their bullets can kill us."

"Shit," Ash cursed and flicked the safety on.

I shook my head, digging my fangs into the man's arm and he screamed in agony again before passing out from the pain. I dropped him to the floor and snarled my rage at the other man.

He was still holding the gun, but his terrified expression told me he wouldn't be testing me the way the other guy had. I crawled back on his hands to put distance between us as magic shot above my head, aimed for Aurelia. She ducked it easily and dove out of the way, sending her own blast of magic at Ronaldo.

My wolf howled a battle cry once again, jumping in front of Aurelia as Ash sent another gust of wind at Ronaldo. "You're all fools. You think you can beat me, but I've already won."

"Look around you," Aurelia scoffed. "Your prisoners are escaping, and your Frankenstein lab is going up in flames. You haven't won anything."

She did blow up his lab. My mate is a badass.

"Frankenstein lab?" Ash asked.

"They had people with no brain function hooked up to machines I think he was trying to create some kind of undead army. It was creepy as fuck." Aurelia shivered.

I nudged Aurelia with my hip and crouched down on the floor. I snarled at Ronaldo as he lifted a hand to shoot magic at us, but Ash blasted him with another gust of air and sent him flying into the wall.

"Get on his back, Princess. We need to go." Ash held his hand out pinning Ronaldo to the wall.

"I can finish this now," Aurelia argued. "If I kill him we can end this."

"This place is about to blow sky high after what you did with your magic. Live to fight another day," Ash gritted out.

I nudged Aurelia with my nose. Fire was getting closer, and we had no idea what horrors she may have missed when destroying the place. My instincts were ruling me, telling me we had to get out of there and fast.

Aurelia ran her hand over the silky fur on my neck and I shivered at her touch. My wolf nearly purred, but we couldn't get complacent. We needed to go.

"Now, Princess," Ash commanded.

Aurelia pulled a face but finally climbed on my back and dug her fingers into the soft fur at my neck. I needed to shift with her when we weren't running for our lives. My wolf loved having her soft hands in his fur.

As soon as she was safely on my back, my wolf leapt over the man lying unconscious on the floor and past a fuming Ronaldo, who was spitting curses at Ash, who still held him immobile with his magic.

We raced from the hall, but it was too late. I skidded to a stop as the building shook violently and a deafening boom filled the space. I crouched as close to the ground as I could get, and Aurelia lay fully down on my back as an explosion tore through the hall, sending us flying.

Flames licked at my fur and a howl of agony tore from my wolf just before I slammed into the wall. Debris and chucks of drywall rained down on my head, knocking me unconscious.

Fuck. I failed my mate and now we were all going to die.

CHAPTER 21

AURELIA

I blinked my watery eyes open to more billowing black smoke and a racking cough exploded from my lungs. Drywall covered my lap, huge chunks of it having fallen on me from the ceiling.

"Fuck. Where's Grey?" I scanned the smoke-filled hall and found the vague outline of my wolf mate against the wall.

I threw the plaster off my lap and crawled over to the wall. Grey was lying on his side a gash on his wolfy snout. His eyes were closed, but his chest was moving with rattling breaths.

I held my hands over his chest and the green glow of my healing magic rushed from my body into his. "Please, please, you have to be okay."

I chanted the words over and over again, praying to the gods that he would be fine but no matter how much magic I poured into him, he wouldn't open his eyes.

I sat back on my heels, staring at him through the smoke until a groan met my ears.

Fuck, Ash is here.

I scanned the room until I found him and rushed over, turning his big body. I almost couldn't move his bulk but after a couple times, I finally rolled him to his back. He groaned again.

"Are you okay? That explosion was horrific," I said.

Ash blinked up at me. He had a gash on his forehead and a piece of debris was sticking out of his side.

"I need a healer," Ash coughed.

"I need to get that piece of wood out of your side, so I can heal you." I shot him an apologetic smile.

This was going to hurt like a bitch, and I needed to be fast before he lost too much blood. I counted down from three in my mind before yanking it out and tossing it aside. Quickly, I placed my hands over the wound, pouring more healing magic into Ash.

He was much better off than Grey. He was at least awake and coherent, but I didn't want to miss anything.

Asher patted my hand, his eyes more focused now that the healing magic was washing through him.

"Where's Grey?" he asked, sitting up.

I pointed to the large, black wolf that was still in a heap and frowned. "He won't wake up. How are we going to get him out of here?"

The heat of the flames around us only grew more intense by the second.

"Easy there, Princess. I'm even stronger than I look." Ash winked at me.

I rushed to Grey and felt his pulse again. It was a little stronger and his breaths weren't rattling the way they had been.

It was a good sign, but I was still worried. His injuries were healed, but he wasn't waking up.

"It will be okay, Princess. He will make it through this." Asher clapped me on the shoulder before bending at the knees and hefting Grey's wolf body over his shoulder.

"We really need to get out of here." I coughed and held my hand over my mouth and nose.

"You first. Grey would kill me if I didn't have your back even if I was lugging his heavy ass at the time."

"You don't have free hands, I do. I can watch all our backs," I argued.

"Fine, but if you tell Grey I let you watch my back, we are going to have a serious problem." He raised a brow at me.

"I won't tell him. Go." I slapped his back.

He took off at a jog and I glanced behind me at the flames. Was someone else back there? Could I dare to hope that Ronaldo was burning in those flames? He was a slippery bastard. He was still alive, I was sure of it.

I followed quickly behind him, sure to keep an eye on our backs. Walls crumbled around us as we ran fire licked at my skin and I winced, but my natural healing repaired the burns almost immediately.

"Almost there!" Asher shouted ahead of me.

Relief flooded me as I coughed again. I heaved in a breath of chemicals and smoke and my lungs burned like they were on fire. They very well could have been with all the toxins in the air.

Asher burst through the doors of the medical unit as another explosion nearly blew us off our feet.

"Why the fuck are they still here?" Ash growled as he surveyed the scene before us.

Shifted animals took on several Fae guards, and Fenrick was off to the side fighting by my father's side as just the two of them battled against six men.

"We all need to get out of here before it's too late," I wheezed.

The air there was much clearer than in the medical unit, and I took in gulps of fresh air.

More guards flooded the space surrounding the group, and my magic pulsed beneath my skin. The shadows writhed over my arms and hands as they swarmed my father and Fenrick.

"Aurelia!" Dan yelled. "They found Aurelia. Retreat."

They were too late though. The guards blocked the door. Shifters snarled and bit the men attacking without mercy in their animal forms as magic flew from the magic users in the room. It was absolute chaos.

No one seemed to hear Dan call for retreat as they continued to fight for their lives, unaware of the dangers they faced. I took a step forward to warn them, but Ash grabbed my arm, keeping me behind him.

"Ronaldo wants your head. He probably sent these guards in so they can kill you," Ash warned and pushed me back behind him.

"I'm not weak, Asher," I growled. "I can take care of myself."

"And Grey will have my head if something happens to you. Just stay behind me while I get you both out."

"I can't promise you that." I shook my head.

I had friends and family out there fighting for their lives and if they needed me, I was going to help them, no matter what Asher said. He knew that as well as I did, if the frown on his face was anything to go by.

"I know, but I had to say it to save my own skin."

We hustled out into the mayhem and dodged the guards. Several rushed us and even with Grey over his shoulder, Ash was able to use elemental magic to gust air at them and throw them against the wall ten feet away.

"Aurelia?" my father shouted.

I turned to him and watched in horror as someone came up behind him with an electrified baton. The man was grinning like an evil mastermind as he swung the baton at my father's head.

I screamed, and my shadows burst from my body, writhing around the room. People froze in confusion instead of getting out of the way of the mass of black that was eating up the prison.

"Run!" I yelled.

Would the shadows let the supernaturals go untouched or was this all going to be a bloodbath? I didn't know. I wasn't in control as shadows wrapped around guards, flinging them in every direction.

The shadows pulsed around the shifters, and I raced to my father as the guard was thrown into the wall with a loud thwack.

"We need to move!" I screamed.

Shadows swirled through the space and finally died down as the guards were all either pinned to the wall or lying in a heap on the floor.

"Princess, what did you do?" Fenrick asked me with wide eyes.

"I may have blown up their lab, and if we don't get out of here soon, that won't be the only thing on fire." I glanced around the room to the door.

Prisoners flooded from the room now that the guards were all taken out. Ash jogged up to my side with Zeke and Dan hot on his heels.

"You were supposed to leave," Ash griped at the men.

"Did you really expect us to just leave the boss behind?" Dan raised a brow.

"Can we argue about this later?" I threw my hands up in frustration.

Plaster and drywall crumbled and fell on my head as we ran for the door. I didn't even notice the guard at the entrance until he was directly in front of me, slashing at me with a sword.

I reared back away from the sword, bending my back. There was a breath of air across my nose, that was how close it got. Fenrick roared behind me and lunged at the guard, but my shadows were already taking care of the man.

They flung him back ten feet into a wall and he smacked his head against it. The crunch that followed turned my stomach. He wasn't dead because he was Fae, but he was going to have some problems if he didn't heal quickly enough.

Arms wrapped around me from behind and I turned sharply to find my father nearby.

"You're okay," he whispered with relief.

"No time for that, Dad. We need to get out of here before the whole place explodes." I grabbed his hand and tugged him along with me, glad to see the people I loved still alive.

"You called me Dad." He swallowed hard.

"I told you I remembered now." I glanced around.

Panic warred inside me as I scanned the doors. There were too many people inside. They needed to run.

"Aurelia? What happened to you?" Fenrick asked, pointing at my side.

I glanced down as I stepped outside into the cool night breeze and gasped. There was something sticking out of my side. Blood oozed from the wound that wouldn't heal because of the foreign object piercing my skin.

How did I miss that?

I dropped to my knees, fire burning in my side and moaned in pain. Someone caught me before I fell completely into the dirt and strong hands cradled my body.

"Where did that come from?" Fenrick whispered as he touched the piece of wood.

I screamed, agony lancing through my side even with the soft brush of Fenrick's gentle touch.

"I didn't even feel it," I gasped. "I don't know."

"We have to remove it, daughter," my father said.

"I know. I just can't," I cried.

Fenrick held my arms to my sides as he cradled me to his chest. "The faster we get it out, the faster you can heal."

I understood that logically, but the pain was making it impossible to see reason as I tried to pull away from him. I didn't want it to come out. It would hurt even more. What if my healing didn't help fast enough?

"I'll heal you the second the piece is out." Fenrick squeezed me tighter.

He kept my arms trapped so I couldn't call my magic.

"No," I said on a moan.

My father's face came into view. "Yes, daughter. You need

to get that wood out, and we need to get back to the Syndicate where it's safe."

"Grey is still unconscious, Princess." Fenrick reminded me. "But I fear trying to sift you with the wood in your wound."

"Aurelia," Ash growled. "I will hold your ass down. You just pulled a piece like that out of me without an argument. Let them do it, or I will force you."

"Fine," I croaked through a dry throat.

I braced myself against Fenrick as Zeke stepped closer. "This will be quick, Princess, I promise."

My vision dotted with white spots as Zeke gripped the piece of wood and didn't even count. My back arched and a scream tore through my lips as he pulled it from me. Blood gushed from the wound, soaking my pants and shirt before healing magic flooded me.

Even with Fenrick's magic flooding me, my eyes rolled into the back of my head. Would his magic be enough... was my last thought before blackness engulfed my vision and I passed out.

CHAPTER 22

GREY

Pain lanced through my body as I shifted back to human. What the hell happened? Blinking my eyes open a sterile white room greeted me.

Where am I? Did Ronaldo catch us?

I panicked when something held my arm down. I turned to find Aurelia's head on my shoulder, sleeping peacefully. Thank the gods she was there and safe. Memories of what happened cleared as I continued to blink away the confusion.

The last thing I remembered was the explosion and debris falling on me.

How did I get here?

I ran my fingers through her hair, and she groaned, shifting her body closer to mine. She was so fucking beautiful it hurt to look at her sometimes.

Now that all the pain was gone, my body felt amazing. Better than it had in days, weeks, months even.

"Grey?" Aurelia asked, blinking her eyes open.

"Hello, mate." I grinned, kissing her forehead.

"You're okay?" she asked, searching my eyes.

"I'm better than okay now that I have you back in my arms. I thought you were dead." I reached out and pulled her body flush with mine in the bed.

"I couldn't get you to wake up. I healed you and you were still unconscious through our escape." She buried her face in the crook of my neck.

"I'm fine, my love." I kissed her temple.

She squeezed me tighter, and my wolf howled in my head. I needed to reconnect with my mate. It had been way too long since we were together. I needed to prove to myself she was really here, alive.

I pulled her onto my chest and kissed down the side of her neck. Aurelia squirmed in my arms. "Grey, what are you doing? You were just unconscious."

"Need you," I growled.

I couldn't get any more words out between kisses than that. My wolf was riding my ass to get closer to her and reconnect on a primal level—the only level he understood. He was all instinct, and that was all that mattered to him.

"I don't think this is a good idea," she moaned, but her hands fisted in my shirt, pulling me closer.

I chuckled before flipping us over so she was on her back. I pinned her to the bed beneath me and stared into her eyes.

"I thought you were dead." I gripped her chin between two fingers.

"I'm right here." She ran her hands up my chest and around my neck and through my hair.

She pulled my head down to meet her lips in a claiming kiss.

I groaned, and my cock hardened against her thigh. This woman was everything. Just pulling me into a kiss could make me hard as stone for her. I had never felt anything like what I felt for her.

Her tongue teased my lips, and I opened immediately to her. Our tongues danced languidly in an exploration of each other.

Breaking the kiss, I trailed my lips down her neck. Her fingers tightened in my hair as I kissed lower. I nipped her collarbone and pulled the strap on her tank top to the side. Her nipples pebbled where my chest was pressed to hers. The only thing between us was her tiny sleep shirt.

"Why do you have clothes on?" I groaned, pulling up the shirt and releasing her breasts.

I licked my lips and reached out, rolling one nipple between my fingers. Her nails dug into my scalp as I leaned forward and took the other nipple in my mouth.

"Grey," she growled.

"You didn't answer my question, my love. I need these off." I untangled her fingers from my hair and sat back on my heels, pulling her up with me.

Her hair was mussed, and her eyes glowed with lust. She was just as hungry for me as I was for her. I tugged the hem of her shirt up and over her head and pressed my lips to hers.

"I'm going to worship every inch of your body before I push inside you and make you come on my cock," I muttered between kisses.

I gripped her hands in mine, and laid her back on the bed, pinning her hands above her head and kissing my way down her chest.

"Keep your hands there or I'm going to edge you so hard, you'll be a sobbing mess, begging me to let you come." I stared into her eyes, waiting for her nod before I let her hands go.

I stroked down her arms with a featherlight touch that had her squirming beneath me, clamping a hand on her hip to still her. I was already hard as granite beneath her, and if she didn't stop moving, I was going to explode.

"Grey, I need you."

"Not yet, mate." I shook my head.

I pressed a kiss to each of her breasts and moved lower nipping at her hipbone on my way to where I really wanted to go. "Spread those pretty thighs for me."

Her legs fell open wide on my command and a strangled sound escaped my throat at how wet she already was through her lace panties. I shifted one hand to a claw and tore them off her, throwing the scraps over my shoulder in my haste.

I breathed deeply through my nose. The scent of her arousal filled the air. My wolf howled in my mind, thrashing to get to his mate and mark her once and for all as ours, but I held him back. This wasn't the time for that.

"You smell like heaven," I said.

I gripped her inner thighs with both hands, holding them down on the bed. Her eyes burned with need as her chest heaved with panting breaths.

Leaning forward, I ran my nose down her thigh slowly, close to her pussy but not where she wanted me most. I wanted to tease her until she couldn't take it anymore, but between her intoxicating scent and beautiful body I didn't know how long I could hold out.

My wolf was still demanding I sink my fangs into her and make her officially ours, but I refused the urge.

"Stop teasing me," she said, frustration lacing her tone as she attempted to wiggle her hips.

She couldn't move though. My fingers dug into her thighs, holding her in place. They were going to leave pretty red marks for a minute when we were done.

My wolf growled in my head as I licked up her pussy to her clit. I sucked her nub into my mouth and stared up at her as her back arched. Her arms, which had been over her head, came down slightly, and I backed away.

"Grey!" she shouted and moved her arms back over head.

"Good girl." I smirked as I licked her again.

Her arms strained with the need to move, but she held them where I commanded. She was obedient even if she was a princess. I sucked her clit between my teeth and she screamed. Her hands fisted the sheets above her head and her shadows swirled around her. She blinked at them and then glanced down at me.

"What are you plotting, love?" I asked, noticing her grin.

Her shadows danced in her eyes. "I think it's time for a little payback."

What is she up to?

Shadows wrapped around my wrists and raced up my arms. They went higher and caressed my shoulders before tweaking my nipples and traveling lower.

"What are you doing, mate?" I asked.

"I told you I was getting payback," she purred.

Her hands were still above her head, but her shadows writhed across my skin and down my abs.

"Aurelia."

"What's wrong?" she asked innocently.

"You know what," I growled, attempting to bat away the shadows making their way down to my already rock-hard cock.

My hands passed right through them and my mate grinned. She loved teasing me in the same way I teased her.

"I have no idea what you're talking about." She grinned.

Her shadows moved down my body and wrapped around my cock, stroking it softly. I pushed two fingers inside her pussy as I unsuccessfully tried to bat away her shadows again. My balls were aching for a release that I refused to give them until I'd wrung a couple of orgasms out of Aurelia.

"Stop," I said in a strangled tone.

"Stop what?" She giggled.

"Don't play games. I'm hanging on by a thread here, mate." I curled my fingers inside her, hitting that spot I knew made her writhe.

"Gods, Grey!" she shouted, her back arching.

Her body convulsed as her shadows became even hungrier, licking and stroking me. Fuck. I wasn't going to last if they kept that up. I gripped her thighs harder and pushed forward, removing my fingers and lining up my cock.

"Is this what you want, my love?" I ran my cock up and down her wet entrance, circling her clit as she came down from her peak.

"Yes!"

Her head thrashed back and forth and her back arched up. Her body shook as I pushed inside her and thrust my cock in her hard and fast. My wolf howled at the connection to our mate, and my balls drew up, ready to explode. I managed to push back my orgasm, stilling inside my mate and holding her down.

She attempted to squirm, but my grip was unrelenting. I couldn't let her move. If I did, this would be over before I was ready, and it had been too long since I'd connected with her for this to end so soon.

"I need a second," I grunted.

"Grey, I need you to move," Aurelia groaned.

I leaned my forehead against hers and took a deep breath, squeezing my eyes closed to calm myself. Her shadows pulsed against my body.

"Call them back, mate. I can't. I'm going to come if you don't pull them back," I grumbled.

If anything, the shadows went crazier than before. They caressed my skin and something wet slid over my nipple. I couldn't hold myself back anymore.

I thrust forward, and Aurelia's fingers tightened in the sheets above her head. Her chest heaved with her panting breaths, and I leaned forward, taking a nipple into my mouth.

"Gods, Grey. I'm gonna come," Aurelia moaned.

"Come for me, mate," I said and bit her nipple.

Her entire body shook as her body milked my cock. I lost all control and pistoned my hips into hers, chasing my own orgasm. My hands tightened on her thighs as I thrust deep inside her for the final time.

Tingles raced down my spine to my balls, and I moaned out her name. My wolf howled in my mind, urging me to mark her for real. Begging me to make her mine. My mouth filled with sharpened fangs, but I refused to mark her for life yet.

I slumped to the mattress next to my mate and pulled her

sated body into my arms, resting my chin on her shoulder, waiting for her to catch her breath.

"I missed you. I thought you were dead." My voice cracked at the end.

"I'm okay, Grey. I promise." She kissed my chest just over my heart. "I'm not going anywhere."

"What happened?" I asked, because that was what I still didn't understand.

How was she there in my arms when I watched her fall into that hole? How had she survived?

"The trees did it to help me get the book," she said simply.

"I'd wondered if it was the trees." I squeezed her tighter.

My mate was amazing, which was a good thing, because she would have to be strong to get through the challenges we still faced.

We'd won the battle, but I had a feeling we wouldn't get through the war unscathed.

CHAPTER 23

AURELIA

I squirmed in Grey's arms. We were back together, and I couldn't help but smile at that, though we still had work to do.

"We need to go," I groaned into his chest.

"Not yet. I have you naked in my arms. I need more time." His arms tightened around me.

"Grey, Ronaldo got away and somehow Malcolm is controlling the human government. We need to make a plan." I wiggled against him.

Bad move. His body hardened against me.

"That's not helping the situation." He grinned.

"Grey, come on." I slapped his chest.

Finally, he let me up and I raced to the bathroom to get ready for the day. I was excited to visit with my friends who'd been imprisoned. I'd seen then as we escaped but hadn't been able to talk to anyone.

Arms wrapped around me as I turned the shower on. "None of that, Grey. We need to call a meeting."

"Fine," he said and stalked from the bathroom.

I hurried through my shower and got dressed. Grey was waiting in the bedroom for me, fully dressed in one of his crisp suits. He looked absolutely delicious, and he was all mine. I strutted up to him and went up on my toes for a kiss.

Grey leaned down, brushing his lips against mine. "If you want us to leave this room, I suggest you not look so sexy when asking for a kiss."

"Fine," I pouted and turned to leave.

Grey gripped my hand and pulled me back into the circle of his arms. He grinned and led me from the room. When we got into the hallway, worried faces looked at us with relief.

"Aurelia," my father breathed.

"Dad," I said, smiling.

His eyes widened at the word and a small grin lit his features with happiness. His eyes misted with tears as I hugged him.

"I thought they were going to kill you in that place." I sniffed.

"Me? I'm stronger than that." He chuckled and squeezed me closer.

Grey's hand was still around my waist. It flexed against my hip, like he was unwilling to let me go. I understood the feeling. I didn't want to let him go either. What would I have done if I thought he was dead?

I couldn't say that I wouldn't be behaving the exact same way. "We need to call a meeting. We need to figure out a way to stop Ronaldo."

"He was in the medical unit with us, right?" Grey asked, frowning.

"He was, but I doubt he was killed in the blast. We just couldn't get that lucky." I rolled my neck back on my shoulders.

I wish he would have died in that explosion.

"You're right." Grey nodded.

He pulled me along behind him to the office that had been my home the last few weeks. He sat in his office chair and pulled me down into his lap.

"Grey," I said, wiggling to stand.

Grey's hands tightened around my waist. He wasn't going to let me up and if I kept wiggling, there would be a bigger problem on his mind.

"Stop, mate. Let me hold you." He pressed a kiss to my neck.

"Okay," I sighed and leaned my back against his chest.

His arms were bands of steel around me, so it really didn't matter if I agreed or not. He was in control.

Dan cleared his throat and turned the volume up on the TV. The explosion was caught on camera along with a flood of inmates leaving the scene. Magic swirled on the screen, and I saw my own image there.

"Supernaturals that were deemed too dangerous caused an explosion at the maximum-security prison outside of Dallas yesterday. The President is about to make a statement shortly."

"Where did they get video?" I asked, straightening in Grey's lap.

"I'm sure they had surveillance cameras all over the prison. They probably took it from there." Grey rested his chin on my shoulder.

I stared at the screen as the building burned and people fled. The words at the bottom of the screen caught my attention.

Many dangerous supernaturals at large in Dallas after grizzly prison break. Death toll is currently unknown.

"Dangerous," I scoffed. "We didn't become dangerous until they made us that way. It's their fault people died."

"I know, love, but they don't see it that way." Grey kissed the side of my neck.

"They can't see past their own fear," my dad said.

"How do we stop this witch hunt?" I asked, and everyone shrugged.

No one knew what to do. It was going to be up to me. I would have to figure this all out. I glanced down at the desk. The gold book was still sitting where I'd left it when we went on the mission to rescue the supernaturals in prison.

Could the book help me with the humans as well as the Council? It couldn't hurt to try.

"I don't know, but we will figure something out." Grey squeezed my hip.

"Shhh," Dan waved a hand at the TV.

The President stood in front of the podium to address the nation. I sat forward, hoping that he wouldn't incite more violence against us, but I wasn't hopeful when I glanced behind him and once again found Malcolm standing there.

"My fellow Americans. It has come to our attention that a tragedy struck just yesterday outside of Dallas. The National Guard has been mobilized to remedy this situation so that the dangerous supernaturals who've committed this egregious act against humanity are swiftly brought to justice."

"That's so much bullshit. What was a crime was the

horrible things they were doing to people inside that place," I said.

Grey shuddered. Had he gotten the same treatment in that place that I did? I glanced at him over my shoulder with concern, but he shook his head. His eyes were haunted.

"I am calling for anyone with information on the whereabouts of the rogue supernaturals to come forward so they can be tried for their crimes."

A picture of me flashed on the screen and I gasped. "What the hell?"

"How did they get a picture of you?" Grey asked.

"This is the mastermind behind the prison break, and she is considered extremely dangerous. Do not approach her. If you see her, call the police immediately. There is a reward for information that leads to her arrest."

"That was my plan," Zeke grumbled.

"And it almost got us all killed." I glared at him.

"And now Aurelia is enemy number-one." Grey tilted his head back and squeezed his eyes shut.

"Did you see Malcolm behind the President again?" I asked, changing the subject.

"Yeah," Zeke sighed. "There has to be a way to stop all this."

"Wait, Malcolm?" Grey asked.

"We think he's controlling the President, but before we got into the prison, we weren't exactly sure how. Now we know that they are testing a mind control serum. They have probably been using it on all the world leaders but for how long?"

Zeke tapped away at his keyboard. "We're safe here for now though, if they don't know where we are. We just need to bide our time and figure out a way to get to Malcolm."

"Malcolm is mine," Grey said, growling.

"It's not about me anymore, Grey. It's about all supernaturals. He needs to be taken out by any means necessary." I shook my head.

I loved the growly, possessive Alpha that wanted to kill anyone who dared to hurt me, but I wasn't a damsel in distress. I was destined to stop this mess and I would, but I would have help. Grey needed to understand that if someone else had the opportunity to take Malcolm out, they had to take it.

We may never get another shot.

"Who is this girl?" the announcer on the TV asked, pulling me from my thoughts.

Another video of me played on the screen, shadows dancing around me and my hair blowing in the wind. That wasn't good.

"I don't know but from that video, she looks like she's a demon. Are demons real?" the other announcer asked with a gasp.

I shook my head. "Fucking idiots."

"The President has a meeting today with the UN to discuss the global supernatural problem." The video cut off and showed the UN building with all the world's top leaders shaking hands.

"Do you see that?" I asked, pointing to Malcolm.

"Fuck," Fenrick said.

"What?" I asked.

"They are all Fae. The men talking with Malcolm are all there to control the human leaders." Fenrick ran a hand down his face.

"It's not just Malcolm using the serum on them?" I asked.

That would make things exceedingly more difficult. How could we free all the world leaders if there were multiple Fae controlling them? The only time they were ever all in the same place was at the UN Council meetings.

"This is a bigger problem than even we realized. How many Fae do they have controlling humans?"

"If I know Ronaldo, he has a back-up for every Fae he has watching the world leaders. He's been planning this too long. He won't take any chance that he could fail," Fenrick said.

"So, then just taking Malcolm out wouldn't work on its own." I slumped back into Grey's chest.

Grey rubbed his thumb in soothing circles over my hip. "We'll figure this out. We don't have any other choice."

"I know, but I can't just sit here doing nothing. The world's leaders are about to hold a meeting deciding the fate of supernaturals, and there's nothing we can do about it. What if they decide to wipe us all out?"

"They probably will try to do just that, but they won't succeed."

"How can you be so sure?" I asked.

"Because even if they knew where this place was, they can't get through my wards with their weapons." Grey shuffled in his seat beneath me.

"Ronaldo could, though. He's been developing more than a mind control serum. The guns that they had pointed at me were Fae made, combining human tech and magic."

"How is that even possible?" Grey asked. "Metal and magic don't mix. Are you sure they were magic?"

"Ronaldo was so smug, telling me how those weapons were strong enough to kill me. I'm not sure how he pulled it off, but there was no iron that I could feel in them. They were magic."

"Either way, they have no idea where we are. If they did,

they would be here instead of calling for blood with their human puppet."

"Right. We don't have to worry about that yet." I turned to Dan. "Is the lockdown still in effect?"

"Yes, no one leaves. We aren't even sending extraction teams because it's too risky." Dan crossed his arms over his chest.

"Good. We were almost at capacity before the prison break, so we probably have even less room now," I said, but my gut sank.

What if there were other innocents out there that we could help? What if more supernaturals were put in a position to be annihilated because we weren't able to provide assistance? What if people died just so we could stay safe? I wasn't sure I could live with myself if I knew people died like that.

"Hey... we will help as many as we can, okay?" Grey squeezed me closer.

"How? This place is full, and we can't let the Council and their weapons find us, or everything was for nothing. All the suffering will be for nothing if we let them find us. It will end in the death and torture of all supernaturals."

I would die before I let that happen.

CHAPTER 24

GREY

I held Aurelia to me, not caring that we were in the middle of a meeting to plan how the hell we were going to stop the Council.

"I think I found a way to get to the President!" Zeke shouted.

"What is it?" Aurelia sat forward, snapping the golden book closed.

"He's going to be at a gala in Dallas tomorrow night. It's a last-minute addition to the war on supernaturals." Zeke frowned.

"There shouldn't even *be* a war on supernaturals. We have lived here for centuries without a problem," I said.

My wolf howled in my mind. We had protected the humans from the worst of our kind, and this was the thanks we got for it. Bullshit fear was the only reason we were being targeted. People turned stupid when they didn't understand something.

"Be that as it may, they are raising money to fund their agenda and let people know they are safe." Zeke shook his head.

"They have been relatively safe from us for *centuries*. We have even protected them from supernaturals that wished them harm. But because they never saw the good, they're focusing on their fear and the fact that we are more than they are."

Dan cleared his throat. "Hate to give an unpopular opinion here, but what happens if we release the President from the mind control and it just makes things worse?"

"What do you mean?" Aurelia asked.

It was nice to see her interacting with Dan after he'd inadvertently gotten her foster mother killed. Or at least that's what she thought. I never thought the two of them would get past that.

"Right now, they're being controlled so they only attack the innocents." He held up a hand when Aurelia opened her mouth to argue. "It is disgusting what the Council is making them do, but what happens if we release that control, and the government goes full Nazi and tries for complete genocide?"

"According to them, we're animals. It wouldn't be genocide but rather eliminating a threat." I shifted in my chair.

Would they really do that? I thought the world had learned from Hitler. That hadn't been good for anyone.

"Are we entirely sure that's not the Council's idea and the humans are just scared and unsure? It could help to get rid of the Fae controlling them." Aurelia tilted her head to the side.

"Do we want to risk it?" Dan asked. "I say we cut the head off the snake. We should be making plans to get rid of the Council before we worry about the humans."

"Okay, I see your point." I nodded. "But we are going to a

full out war with the Council? How are we going to fight the humans after a bloody war?"

"We may not have to if these aren't their actual policies." Dan shrugged.

"Then why not get the mind control broken and then go after the Council?" Aurelia asked.

"If we go after the humans first, then we may be fighting a war on two fronts. One against the humans and one against the Council. It would spread us too thin, and we don't have much of an army as it is."

He wasn't wrong. Our army was small and consisted of mercenaries and people with not a lot of discipline. The people who worked for me were highly trained, but there weren't a lot of them. The Council had taken over the Shadow King's army on top of having their own guards. We would be screwed if we had to fight both the Council and the humans.

"He may have a point," I sighed.

"What?" Aurelia sat forward and turned to me sharply. "They shouldn't lose their free will. If we can stop the mind control, maybe they'll realize we aren't the enemy they think we are."

Zeke's hand flew over his keyboard. "With all due respect, Princess, that's a bit naïve. No, they shouldn't be without their free will, but do you honestly think their gratitude will outweigh their fear?"

Aurelia deflated. Her shoulders slumped. "You're right."

I glared at the rider for upsetting my mate. She didn't deserve the *naïve* comment. She was the one who was going to save us all. The pressure of that knowledge weighed heavily on her. I wished I could take that burden from her, but it wasn't my burden to bear. It killed me.

"I agree the fear will still make the human government take action against the threat. Even if the President doesn't agree about us being a danger, he will be pressed to act against us no matter what."

Aurelia moved to stand, but my arms tightened around her, unwilling to let her go. "I don't care if they come for us. We shouldn't let them continue to be controlled."

"You're too good for supernaturals, love." I kissed her cheek. "They made us their enemies. I would just assume deal with one opponent at a time."

"So, we are imprisoning them the way they are doing to us? How is that right?" She crossed her arms over her chest and sat stiffly on my lap since I refused to let her move.

My wolf was being a possessive fucker. He didn't like the idea of my mate moving to anyone else in the room despite knowing they were no threat to our claim on her.

"We are only holding off on helping them until we neutralize the bigger threat, love. They will get their free will back, but I don't think it's wise to do it yet."

Ash took a step forward. "With all due respect, I agree with the princess. They may only be acting in a way the Council wants them to and may be an asset in the war against the Council."

Aurelia glanced over her shoulder at me with a glare. She agreed with him clearly, but what would happen if they were even more aggressive in their need to get rid of us or test on us? It could have been ten times worse.

I sat back and thought about his statement. The Fae

Council was trying to eradicate us and there wasn't a whole lot we could do about it without getting rid of them, which we still didn't know how we would get that accomplished. Maybe it would be best to get rid of Malcolm's mind control and see where the chips fell with the humans.

"Okay, I think we should take the chance and stop the mind control on the President. They could be an asset and honestly, my kind-hearted mate is right. No one should have their free will stripped from them."

Aurelia turned to me with wide eyes and smiled. My wolf preened that she was no longer mad at us.

"Now that's settled, let's get that information on where the President will be tomorrow." Aurelia clapped her hands.

She really was the best of us despite the burden Fate had rested on her shoulders. I couldn't believe this woman was mine.

"He'll be at a fancy restaurant downtown campaigning for the arrest of all supernaturals and calling for more regulations. That's what the gala is raising money for," Zeke growled.

"They are literally raising money to have us as lab rats that they can study to make super-human soldiers." I shook my head.

It was disgusting. How could they do this to people who had never harmed them? We'd lived among them and protected them. Why was it now that they knew we existed that they had a problem with their neighbors and friends.

We had been part of many communities and had human friends, but just because they now knew we were different, we couldn't be trusted.

"I'm guessing that's exactly what the human government wants, but the Council is controlling how much information they get." Zeke typed a few things on his keyboard as he spoke.

"How are we getting into the gala?" Aurelia asked.

She leaned back into me again, finally not trying to leave my arms, which my wolf loved. He didn't want his mate far from him after the distance while we were in prison.

"I've already hacked the guest list and gotten all of us invites under fake names. There's only one problem." Zeke glanced around at all of us.

"What is it?" I asked pulling Aurelia back.

"Aurelia is enemy number-one." Zeke raised an eyebrow at her.

"Shit," she groaned and leaned her head back on my shoulder.

"What are we going to do?" I asked as the Shadow Queen walked in with a glint in her eyes.

"I have a talent that may be able to help with that," the queen said with a smirk.

"Mother? You can help?" Aurelia perked up.

"I have exceptional glamour. Even better than what you do for your wings." She glanced pointedly at Aurelia's glamoured wings.

She still hadn't learned to use them effectively, but when she was taught to hide them from the world at a young age, I couldn't blame her for that. She needed to learn though.

We would have to make it a priority after the war. She needed to be strong to be the queen. She was already the strongest woman I'd ever met after the things she'd endured, but I needed her at one hundred percent.

"Can you change all our appearances?" I asked.

That would be extremely useful and help us get into the gala and kill Malcolm, eliminating the mind control on the President.

"I can only do four at a time. I have tried more, but it ended badly. Pick your top four." The queen eyed us all.

"Well, obviously, I'm going," Aurelia said, and I growled.

I scooped her up in my arms and stomped through the office and into the hall.

"Aurelia, please. Don't do this. They want you dead more than anyone. I can't lose you." I cupped her cheeks and backed her up against the wall.

"I have to, Grey. I can't let this happen. They need to be stopped. Malcolm needs to be stopped." She shook her head and tried to pull away.

I wouldn't let her go, though. I couldn't. She was mine. I couldn't handle it if something terrible happened to her. My wolf would go rabid. He would lose his shit, and we would have to be put down if anything happened to her. I would never be the same.

"But you don't. You could stay here safe until the actual war comes to pass. You're the one destined to end this madness. If something happened to you, then it could destroy everything," I said. "It would destroy me."

I pulled her close and pressed my lips to hers. I couldn't survive without her.

All I could hope for was that if something happened to her, I died too. My life was over without her.

CHAPTER 25

AURELIA

The dress that they helped me into was too tight. I could barely breathe through the corset strapped around my torso.

"How the hell am I going to fight in this?" I asked, turning to the men in the room who all stared at me like I was a piece of meat.

"Stop it!" Grey barked, glaring at the others. "You're making her nervous."

"They're making me uncomfortable, not nervous." I stepped into the entryway.

"Well, they need to stop that too," Grey grumbled. "You're mine. They need to stop looking at you like that."

Grey wrapped his arm around my waist as we all made our way to the parking garage. Zeke, Ash and Dan followed behind us. My mother had glamoured us so everyone we met would see something different, but we still saw each other as we truly were.

"You remember the plan?" Grey asked me as he helped me into the limo.

"We make plans all the time, but they seem to go to shit every time."

"I know, but we don't know exactly what we're walking into, so I wanted to make sure." He settled into the seat next to me and rested his hand over the form-fitting dress on my thigh.

"I get it." I sat back with a huff.

What was I doing? Was I going to get us all killed thinking that I could take Malcolm out? He deserved it, and I wanted nothing more than to end him for the hell he'd put us through.

It was more than that though. He was behind the human government imprisoning and testing supernaturals. I would see him dead before this war was over.

We arrived at the red carpet and the guys all piled out of the car before Grey reached a hand out for me to take. My form-fitting emerald dress flared out at the bottom and my hair was done in an elegant up-do on top of my head.

"You look beautiful, love," Grey whispered in my ear.

"You look good yourself, but we aren't here to have fun." I scanned the carpet behind him.

I didn't see Malcolm but that didn't mean he wasn't puppeteering the president. Grey wrapped an arm around my waist and led me through the doors into the ballroom.

The entire room was filled with an opulence that I wasn't used to. The other guys fanned out around the room, but they kept their eyes on us as we swept through the area.

"The President isn't here yet. He will probably be the last to arrive and surrounded by security," Grey muttered.

"So, what do we do then?" I asked, sucking my bottom lip into my mouth.

"We can dance. It will give us a better view of the room and we can see if we can get eyes on Malcolm."

"What if he doesn't show up?" I asked, worried.

Everything hinged on Malcolm being at that gala with the President, but what if he wasn't? What would we do to stop the atrocities happening to the supernaturals?

I would have done anything to stop the crazy madness. I couldn't stop anything if Malcolm didn't show up, though.

Grey twirled me around the dance floor, and I scanned the room, but no matter how hard I looked, I didn't see the slimy fucker, Malcolm. The doors to the ballroom opened, and a flood of men in black suits surrounded someone in the middle.

The President was there, his wife on his arm in a flowing, royal blue gown. She looked elegant and sophisticated. Too bad her husband might have been a world class asshole.

"Let's see if we can get close to them," I whispered.

"No need. Zeke moved around the seating chart online and got us a spot at his table." Grey smirked.

"Of course, he did. That man never does anything halfway." I shook my head.

They announced dinner being served and Grey led me to the table and pulled my chair out for me. I sat down primly next to the First Lady and my eyes widened at Grey. Zeke really wasn't playing around when he set this all up.

"Hello." The First Lady nodded to me before turning back to her husband.

"This is such a great cause. I'm so pleased to be able to donate," I said loudly.

The words tasted like bile on my tongue. It was not a great cause. It was a death sentence for so many of us, but I needed to get the President's attention.

"I'm glad to meet a fellow American who believes in this amazing cause." The President nodded.

"Oh, yes, I anxiously await the day that we have them all rounded up," Grey said smoothly.

"Yes, the recent devastating attack on the prison here has set us back slightly, but they will be found and brought to justice for their crimes," the President said.

Their *crimes*. He'd really said that, and I didn't see Malcolm anywhere in the room. How far away did the mind control work? Was it the mind control serum, or did the President really believe what he was saying?

"The extremists say that the prison was set to explode anyway, and that it was just a safe place to round up supernaturals so they could exterminate them," Grey commented.

The President's eyes flashed with a warning as he narrowed his eyes at Grey. "That's ridiculous. We are just protecting the American people from dangerous beings who shouldn't be here in the first place."

"And rightly so," I said, glaring at Grey to cool down.

He was going to blow our cover if he wasn't careful. We hadn't found Malcolm, and it looked like this whole mission was for nothing anyway because the President fully believed in his prejudice.

What the fuck were we supposed to do now? I locked gazes with Zeke and widened my eyes at him. The President caught on quickly and glanced between me and Zeke. I was the only one really in disguise since I was enemy number-one.

The President stood up so fast his chair toppled to the ground and he pointed at Zeke and Ash. "They are supernatural. They are the ones who blew up the prison. Get them!"

A hand clamped around my arm and dragged me up out of my seat. I screamed in the Secret Service agent's face before cocking my arm back and punching him.

My knuckles cracked against his nose, and I shook my hand out. I spun around to find Grey. His body vibrated, his wolf close to the surface. Claws replaced his hands as he stared down the two men approaching him. They were also wearing dark suits like the Secret Service.

"If you resist, it will be worse for you," the President announced loudly.

"It can't get much worse than the Council trying to blow us all up," I sneered.

"That's a lie." The President slammed his fist down on the table.

The other people backed away from the spectacle, leaving the five of us alone with the President and his Secret Service agents.

"It's not. We were all locked in that hellhole, tested on and tortured!" I yelled.

I needed the people in that room to hear me, but as I stared into the President's eyes, they were clear. He wasn't being controlled. He actually believed in what he was doing. That was even worse than the alternative.

No one would be safe in the mortal world with the human government actually out to get us. Arms wrapped around me from behind, squeezing me like a vise. The man lifted me from my feet, and I kicked back into his shin with my pointy heel. A bellow of rage filled the room as Grey slammed a clawed fist into one of the men before him.

My shadows pulsed beneath my skin as my magic writhed. It wanted out. It wanted to protect me from the threat. If I used my magic against them, I would be playing directly into their hands and showing them that we were monsters.

That wouldn't help matters at all. All it would do is create more fear. It would cause more chaos. I didn't want to be the reason for that. Shadows swirled over my arms angrily. People gasped and backed away from me.

"That's her, the woman that blew up the prison," several people whispered.

Fuck. The shadows were a dead giveaway.

"Get her!" the President roared.

Suddenly, Zeke was in front of me. I hadn't even seen him move.

"What are you doing?" I whispered at his back.

"You have to be protected." He grunted as magic filled his palms.

"Zeke, no. We can't use magic against them, or we are exactly what they think we are," I hissed.

"We are protecting ourselves. That's all we've ever done. It's why we hid for centuries among them. I'm not letting them take you to Ronaldo."

"You can't use your magic," I growled.

"Fine." He dropped the magic but didn't move out of my way.

I glanced around the room. Grey was fighting against two Secret Service agents, but they were no match for him. He took them down with his fists alone, but his claws punctured his palms and blood dripped from them.

"We need to go. Right now!" Grey bellowed.

Zeke backed me up to Grey, and the others created a protective barrier around me as Zeke put up a shield. They couldn't get to us through his ward.

"Do not let them leave." The President took a step forward. "They need to pay for their crimes."

Several of the agents pulled guns and pointed them at us. Still, Zeke kept backing us toward the door. They were all protecting me, and I hated it.

They needed to protect themselves too, but would it do any good to tell them that? A gust of wind blew through the room and pushed the guards back. I peered over at Ash with a raised brow.

"I said no magic," I growled.

The agents lifted their semi-automatics at us. "Just surrender and no one gets hurt."

"We aren't doing anything. We didn't do anything to deserve this treatment in the first place. Just let us go." I shook my head.

"Don't move," another agent said.

He pointed his gun at my head, ready to take me down by any means necessary. If those guns housed Ronaldo's deadly bullets we were all fucked.

Zeke's magic flared as he once again stepped in front of me, blocking me from the agents. A loud shot cracked through the air, and arms grabbed me from behind, turning me into a hard chest and spinning me around.

I screamed and thrashed in those arms, but Grey's warmth

soothed me. I peeked around him just in time to witness Zeke fall to the ground in a puddle of blood.

No. Not Zeke. As much as he's pissed me off, I didn't want to lose my friend.

I lunged for Zeke and my magic flared even as Grey held me back.

"I know, love, I know. But his sacrifice will be for nothing if we don't leave now." Grey lifted me off my feet and threw me over his shoulder as he raced to the door. The others shot magic at the agents until we were on the other side.

Tears poured down my cheeks as we made our way outside into the humid Dallas air. Zeke was gone. I turned to Ash. His face was stricken but determined at the same time.

"We can mourn him later, Aurelia. We have to go. That's what he would want."

My heart broke as we ran. How could we just leave one of our own behind?

Dan ran next to me. "Live to fight another day, Princess."

Yeah, live to fight another day. But how many of those did I really have left?

Printed in Great Britain
by Amazon